COSMIC CONSPIRACY

A MAGICAL MANE MYSTERY
BOOK EIGHT

STELLA BIXBY

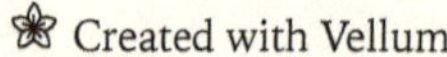 Created with Vellum

For Nolan. I Finally Added Aliens.

CAST OF CHARACTERS

Ellie - Main Character

Penelope - Ellie's Pet Pig

Mona - Ellie's VW Microbus

Esme - Ellie's Grandmother

Emily/Miley - Ellie's Mother

Xander - Warlock

Jake - Cliff Haven Police Chief/Emily's High School Sweetheart

Bex - Ellie's Best Friend/Works at Katie's Café

Katie - Married to Earl/Own's Katie's Café & Theater

Fran - Coupled with Amy/Own's Fran's Fabric & Feed

Amy - Coupled with Fran/Own's Amy's Antiques

Nancy - Married to Hank/Own's Nancy's Nails

Renée - Widowed/Grand Witch of the States

Andrea - Ellie's Magical Guardian

Gerald - Xander's Father

Eloise - Ellie's Sister

Mrs. Wix - Xander's Mother

Gus - Local Townsperson

Marty - Local Townsperson

Deb - Jake's Partner on the Police Department

Jasmine - Gus's daughter

Gorvich - Grandmaster of the Alien Cohort

IN THE LAST BOOK . . .

In *Jamboree Justice*, the previous book in the Magical Mane Mystery Series, Ellie went to Colorado to help clear her mother's name in a murder investigation.

It was there she found out she had a sister and that her mother didn't remember anything about her because Xander's father had cast a memory-erasing spell.

Now, Ellie and Xander are waiting not-so-patiently for an answer from Xander's father on whether he'll accept Ellie's healing powers and take away the memory-erasing spell.

See what he says by turning the page . . .

"Do we have a deal?" Xander held out his hand for his father to shake.

I sucked in a breath. The hospital machines beeps echoed into the silent room, ricocheting off the hard floor and the white walls.

If Gerald agreed to restore my mother's memories, my entire life would change. I'd have my mother back. She could tell me who my father was. I'd even have a little sister.

"I'll have to think about it," Gerald finally said.

"You'll have to think about it?" Xander's voice bordered on frantic. "We don't have time for you to think about it."

"I know what my timeline looks like," Gerald said before his body jolted into a coughing fit. I hurried over to hand him his hospital-issued water bottle.

"Just let me heal you," I said, stepping forward. "Even if you don't restore my mother's memories, let me heal you."

"What's going on in here?" A woman I'd seen in Xander's family photo walked through the door and past the privacy curtain, stealing Gerald's chance to answer my plea. She had Xander's dark brown eyes, thick wavy brown hair, and her magical aura was more prominent than I'd ever noticed on a witch. Xander's mother commanded attention, both with her voice and her presence.

"Did you not hear me? I asked what is going on in here," she said, staring at Xander.

He looked torn. With his mother in the room, he was likely thinking about how his father had created an illegitimate child with my mother.

Yes, my sister—Eloise—was my boyfriend's sister, too. Ugh.

"Xander wanted to introduce me to the famous Ellie Vanderwick—his girlfriend?" Gerald smiled teasingly while looking at the two of us.

Xander glanced at me, causing the heat to rise in my cheeks. I gave him a slight nod. "We haven't discussed it, but something like that."

My heart fluttered.

"I'm delighted to meet you," Xander's mother said formally. "You may call me Mrs. Wix."

I shook her hand. "It's nice to meet you, Mrs. Wix."

She studied me up and down. If only I'd have dressed nicer. She wore cream wide-legged trousers with heels, a silky blush sleeveless blouse, and carried what a designer purse. Meanwhile, I wore black yoga pants, a cotton tank top, and tennis shoes and carried my worn leather satchel.

"Did you really bring her here to meet us?" Mrs. Wix

asked Xander when she had finished with her visual assessment. "Or did you want her to heal your father?"

Wow, nothing got past this woman. Perhaps she already knew about Gerald's affair with my mother. On the other hand, she likely didn't know about Eloise because Gerald hadn't even known about Eloise.

"I offered," I said when Xander didn't speak up.

"And?" Mrs. Wix glanced at Gerald. By the tone of her voice, I couldn't tell whether she wanted me to heal him.

"I said I would think about it," Gerald said. "And I will."

Mrs. Wix nodded once, then turned to Xander and me. "I'm sure your father will let you know when he decides."

"But—"

A mere raise of his mother's eyebrow cut Xander's rebuttal off. "He will tell you of his decision once it is made. Now, you may stay and visit as we haven't seen you in ages. Or, if you intend on pushing the issue of healing and whatever else I suspect you're not telling me, you may leave."

I didn't know what to say, so I simply avoided his mother's gaze and inspected the floor tiles, silently promising myself I'd wash my dirty tennis shoes the moment I got home.

"Ellie's been solving a murder case all weekend. I'm sure she'd like to go home."

His mother mumbled something under her breath, but I didn't quite catch what she said.

"Liz, be nice," Gerald whispered.

She made herself busy rearranging the cup and tray on his hospital table.

I looked up at Xander, but his gaze was on his mother. If looks could kill, Mrs. Wix would have been dead.

"I'll walk Ellie out, then come visit," Xander said.

"Goodbye, Ellie," Gerald said, his words heavy with emotion. "It was a pleasure meeting you."

Mixed emotions coursed through my body. He wasn't only saying see you later. He was saying goodbye forever. He had no intention of allowing me to heal him.

"Likewise," I said, flashing him a smile. While Mrs. Wix had her back to me, I mouthed, "Think about it, please."

Gerald gave me a small smile.

"Mom?" Xander said.

"Oh, yes. Goodbye, Ellie. Do tell your grandmother hello for me."

Her words stopped me in my tracks. "My grandmother is dead."

She finally turned around. "As I well know."

Xander sighed. "Mom can communicate with ghosts. I assume your grandmother is a ghost?"

I nodded.

"She's told me even more about you than Xander has," Mrs. Wix said, her face still neutral and cold. "Which isn't saying much, but it's something."

"I'll tell her you say hi," I said, uncertain how she'd spoken to Esme when I didn't think Esme couldn't leave my property. "It was nice meeting you."

She mumbled something else I couldn't hear as Xander squeezed my hand and led me out the hospital room door.

2

<hr>

Once in the hallway, I wrapped my arms around his waist and pushed my cheek to his chiseled chest.

He laid his head on top of mine and pulled me closer to him. "I'm sorry. I thought he'd do it. I thought even without the healing, he'd do it. But he's a coward and a liar and—"

"Shhhh," I said. "He's your father."

Xander hugged me tighter to him, and I melted a bit more.

When his body stopped jolting with sobs, he lifted his head and wiped the tears from his cheeks. "You know what? We'll do it ourselves. We'll find someone else who can reverse the spell. I'm sure someone can do it. It might take longer than if Gerald did it, but we'll figure it out together, okay? I know we can."

"Let's talk about that later. Right now, you need to go in there and be with your father before he dies."

"But—"

"No buts. Go in there and get caught up. I'm going back to Iowa. If he changes his mind about the healing, you know how to contact me."

"Um, except your phone is out of service," he said.

"Right. It broke. I'll get a new one as soon as I get back."

"How will you get back without Mona?"

I smiled. "I'll teleport."

"Are you sure you can do it? Andrea will kill me if something happens to you. It's a pretty big distance."

"I can do it," I said. "My magic is getting stronger."

He bent down, kissed me gently, then pulled me in for another big hug.

I didn't want to leave. I could have stayed in his arms for hours. But Mona and my friends had probably already gotten home by now. And though I knew my friends would care for Penelope, she preferred me to be home with her.

"I'll see you soon," I whispered.

He kissed me on my forehead, then backed up with a smile. "Very soon."

I started down the hospital hallway to the bathroom. I couldn't disappear where nurses, doctors, and patients could see me.

Before I walked through the door, I looked back to find Xander watching me walk away.

We waved before I ducked inside.

Thankfully, the bathroom was empty. I had to do this quickly before anyone walked in.

I reached for the edges of magic, closed my eyes, and

focused on my house. Within seconds, I'd teleported from Denver, Colorado, to Cliff Haven, Iowa.

A scream startled me as my feet contacted my kitchen floor.

My first thought was someone had found another body.

I turned to find who was screaming and saw Katie sitting at the island clutching her chest.

Penelope oinked with excitement at my presence.

"You scared the living daylights out of me," Katie said.

Relief flooded through me that there wasn't another body on my property. I'd just solved one case and was not looking forward to another anytime soon.

"Sorry," I said. "I didn't know you'd be here, or I'd have landed in my bedroom."

"I don't know that you coming down the stairs would have been any less startling," Katie laughed. She had bags under her eyes and wore the same leggings and blouse combo she'd been wearing when I saw her leaving Colorado in Mona with the rest of our friends.

"I figured Andrea would be here," I said. Andrea was my magical guardian—assigned to me because I was next in line to become the Grand Witch of the States.

"She was but got called away on some business," Katie said. "I told her I'd look out for you."

"And she was okay with that?"

"I think whatever she had to do was pretty important."

I nodded. "Well, thanks for hanging out."

"My pleasure," Katie said. "Was everything okay with Xander?"

"His dad—Gerald—is dying," I said. "We tried to

convince Gerald to reverse the spell on Emily's memory, but he refused. I even offered to heal him, but I guess he would rather die than let whatever secret Emily has about him come out."

"Must be some secret," Katie said.

"How long have you been here?" I opened the fridge and remembered I'd meant to go to the store before I'd made a trip to Colorado.

"Only a couple of hours," she said. "Why don't we go to the café and get dinner?"

"That sounds amazing," I said. "Let me change, and then we can go."

I hurried up the stairs, and Penelope charged up after me. She was good at going up the stairs, but her little piggy legs weren't made for going back down.

The lilac wreath on my bedroom door was as lovely as ever, the real petals never wilting. My room was exactly as I'd left it—messy.

I tidied up a bit before digging for something clean to wear. I'd been in a massive state of depression after seeing Xander with my missing mother. I couldn't remember the last time I'd done laundry.

"What are you looking for?" An ethereal voice came from behind me. I didn't have to turn around to know who was talking.

"Clean clothes," I said to Esme—my grandmother, who was also a ghost. "Do you know where I could find any?"

"Keep digging," she said. "I think there are some in the very back."

I pushed my way into the massive closet. "Mrs. Wix told me to tell you she said hi."

"Lizzy told you to tell me hi?" My grandmother's laugh widened the smile on my face. "I'm surprised she spoke to you now that you and Xander are officially an item."

"Why is that?" I opened a tote in the depths of the closet, trying to find something to wear but coming up empty-handed.

"Xander is her precious baby boy," Esme said. "She has hated every girl he's brought home."

"Including me?" I replaced the lid and walked out. "I didn't see any clothes in there."

"She knows practically nothing about you," Esme said. "And I was kidding. There aren't clothes in there."

I put my hands on my hips. "Where are they really?"

She was as translucent and beautiful and ornery as always. "In your dresser, silly girl."

My stomach growled as I pulled on a new pair of jeans and a T-shirt. "Why hasn't Xander said anything about me?"

"It seems you might be the special one."

My chest expanded. "Special?"

"He probably feels rather protective of you. Especially since he was your guardian."

"You know Mrs. Wix," I said. "How should I handle her?"

"Kill her with kindness," Esme said. "It's the only thing she'll allow. She comes across as a tough old witch, but she has a kind heart and an incredible sense of loyalty."

"Kill her with kindness?" I asked. "Sounds brutal, but I'm sure I can do that."

"You'd be surprised how well the tactic can work in all sorts of situations."

I liked to think of myself as always being kind, but I could definitely ramp it up a bit. Especially in the presence of someone who made me want to disappear into a hole.

"After you eat, I want to hear about your trip," Esme said. "And I must tell you, it's good to have my happy Ellie back."

I smiled at her. "It's good to be back."

<hr>

3

Though I was famished, I needed to replace my phone before we could eat. That way, Xander could contact me.

"Well, well, well, look who's here," Fran said with a smile from behind the small counter. Fran's Feed, Fabric, and Fones—the Fones being the latest part of her business—was on the opposite side of the square from Katie's Café. It was a darker building with few windows that smelled like hay and other animal supplies.

"I'm glad you all made it home," I said. "And right back to work, huh?"

"I had to make sure everything was in shape after I'd been gone," Fran said.

"Don't trust your staff?" Katie teased.

"No one's going to care for your business like you do," Fran said.

"Bex does a pretty good job over at the café," Katie said.

I couldn't wait to see Bex. She was my best friend and the café manager.

"What can I do for you?" Fran asked.

A cat rubbed against my leg. I gathered it up in my arms and let it knead biscuits on my shoulder. "I need a new phone. Mine broke."

"How about a burner?" Fran said. "They could come in handy with a job like yours."

"A therapeutic recreation specialist?" I asked, knowing she was talking about the crime solving, not my actual business.

"Aren't the criminals the ones who usually buy the burner phones?" Katie asked.

Fran replaced the cheap-looking phone in hard plastic wrapping to the pegboard wall behind her where she had only two of the phones total. "Okay, not a burner phone."

"I want to replace mine with the same one I had," I said. "A smart one, but it doesn't have to be fancy or anything."

"Give her the fancy one," Katie said, then looked at me. "You need all the bells and whistles you can get to manage your business, your cases, and becoming Grand Witch."

She had a point. "She's right. Give me the best you have."

Fran did her thing with the phone, getting it all set up with whatever cloud backup I may have had while I looked around the store with the kitty still kneading and purring on my chest.

"Who in the world would need this much neon green

rope?" I asked, finding a spool almost as big as the big round hay bales.

"It goes faster than you'd think," Fran said from the front counter, her voice echoing through the large building. "We have all sorts of colors, keep going down that aisle."

I walked back into the recesses of the building seeing similar rolls of pink, purple, red, orange, and blue. At the end of the row was a door leading into the fabric room. I'd never been inside. I wasn't much of a crafty person.

"All ready for you," Fran shouted.

I hurried back to the front where I found Katie wearing a big straw cowboy hat and aviator sunglasses. "Think I could get away with this?"

"Maybe if you were planning on fixing some fences and going on a cattle drive," Fran said.

Katie pulled off the sunglasses and rolled her eyes. "You're no fun."

Fran didn't seem to care. "Looks like that kitty likes you."

"Does it have a name?" I asked, petting its soft fur. It had stopped purring and kneading and was now fast asleep in my arms.

"Nah, they're barn cats. I don't name 'em." Fran held out my phone.

I gave the kitty one more snuggle and put it on top of a stack of horse blankets, where it spun around twice then curled into a ball.

"Thank you," I said, taking the phone.

"It should have everything on it your old phone had,"

Fran said. "Weren't you worried you'd lost your pictures or something?"

My heart sped. I thought all my pictures of Penelope and me would be totally gone. "Did you get them back?"

"You must have set up the cloud after all," Fran said, navigating to the photos app.

All of the photos were there. My words caught in my throat.

"Aw, don't cry," Fran said, but she was smiling as big as Katie.

"Thank you so much," I said, handing her my debit card.

She rang it all up for me and put the chargers and the box in a bag which I promptly slipped into my satchel.

"See you later," Katie said. "And get some rest. The shop will be here in the morning."

Fran shooed us out the door.

4

The parking outside Katie's Café was packed with cars, SUVs, and shiny pickup trucks with massive tires. Inside, it was full of families sharing dinner and groups of teenagers hunched over their homework.

Katie and I sat in the back at the staff table. It was a habit since I'd moved to Cliff Haven and become a waitress at the café. Plus, Katie owned the place.

Bex, my best friend and the manager slash head server, emerged from the kitchen holding two plates of hot sandwiches. "I'll be right there." She wore black bell-bottom jeans and a yellow peasant blouse and had her hair in long black twists.

"No rush," Katie said to Bex.

My stomach grumbled in disagreement.

"I'll get us some drinks," Katie said. "What would you like?"

"I can get them," I said.

"You've had a long few days. Let me."

"Water would be great."

She hurried off to get me some water while I checked the new phone.

There were no messages from Xander.

"How's my bestie doing?" Bex said, sliding into the booth beside me and wrapping her arms around my neck. "I missed you."

"I was only gone a couple of days."

"And where exactly did you go?"

I suspected Earl—Katie's husband—had informed her of my absence and how I'd taken Katie with me.

"Colorado," I said. "It was a last-minute thing. They needed some help solving a murder."

"And they called you? Wow."

"Something like that." I laughed. "Everything worked out all right. We caught the murderers. Three women. Enemies brought together to destroy a cheating man."

"Sounds like a country song."

We laughed.

"I also found my mother," I said. "Long story short, she doesn't remember Cliff Haven, magic, or me."

Bex gasped. "What? How?"

"I'll fill you in when we have more time to chat," I said. "Oh, and I have a little sister."

Her eyes widened. "Did you meet her?"

"Briefly," I said. "She's sassy."

"Good for her," Bex said. She stood as Katie returned. "What can I get the two of you to eat? The special tonight is the French Dip with fries."

"Mmm," I said. "I'll take that."

"Me too," Katie said. "And some ranch, please."

"Ooh, for me too," I said.

"Will do," Bex said and walked into the kitchen.

I sipped my water. My teleportation only slightly diminished my energy, which meant my magic was getting stronger. Finally.

"Where's Earl tonight?" I asked, but before Katie could reply, an older man burst through the front door wearing nothing but a pair of tightie-whities and what looked like a court-issued ankle monitor.

"They're coming for all of us!"

Several people gasped as another older man—this one fully clothed—burst in behind him. "They're not going to hurt anyone."

Katie hopped to her feet. She looked around at the panicked customers. "Everything's okay. Keep eating." She put her arm around the nearly nude man's shoulders and tried to lead him outside, but he wasn't having it. "Gus, what are you talking about?"

"The aliens are coming to get us! You'll see! They'll probe everyone!"

"They don't probe people," the other man yelled at Gus. "Stop spreading these lies."

"It might be a good idea to put on more clothes to protect yourself," Katie said.

The teenagers by the door snickered.

"Are you laughing at me?" Gus spun out of Katie's arms, past the man yelling at him, and marched over to the teenagers' table. "You think I'm just some crazy old man in my underwear?"

"Looks that way to me," a boy wearing a letterman

jacket said, making his friends laugh.

Gus narrowed his eyes and leaned in closer. "Why do you think I'm only in my underwear?"

"Because you weren't brave enough to go streaking completely naked?"

Gus slammed his fist on the boys' table. The boy's confidence faltered slightly.

"These are special alien-detracting underwear. And since you've been such a little twerp, I'm not giving you a pair from my secret stash."

"I don't think anyone wants a pair of your underwear," Katie said, glancing at me and mouthing, "Help me."

I hurried over, unsure where to put my hands since his back was covered in hair and his shoulders were sweaty.

But before I could decide, the other man grabbed the waistband of Gus's underwear and pulled, effectively giving Gus a massive wedgie and sending them both toppling to the floor.

Katie groaned.

The teenagers were on their feet chanting, "Fight, fight, fight!"

"Get him, Marty," Letterman boy said. "Kick his—"

"Whoa, whoa, whoa," I said, stopping him. "You need to sit down and watch your language."

"You need to mind your own business," Letterman said, taking a step toward me.

I let my hair change from its normal white to a flaming red and said, "Sit down, now."

Like most of the town, he probably knew I was magical and that my hair changed color, but seeing it like that would probably startle most people.

He stumbled back and sat at the table, though he didn't bother to wipe the glare off his face.

When I turned to the pile of old men, they were throwing fists as Katie tried desperately to get them to stop.

I was about to jump in when Big Charlie came storming from the kitchen with Little Charlie on his heels.

Big Charlie pulled Marty off Gus with one hand to the collar of his jacket while Little Charlie—apparently stronger than he looked—held Gus back.

"You two need to quit fighting and get out of this café," Big Charlie bellowed.

Marty glanced at Big Charlie with fear in his eyes. "Okay, I'll leave. We can hash this out somewhere else."

"There's nothing to hash out," Gus yelled. "Stay away from me with your alien-loving mumbo jumbo, or you'll regret it."

The two Charlies practically tossed the men outside while the teenagers stood and cheered.

The rest of the patrons returned to their dinners as if nothing had happened, though I was sure they'd be talking about this incident for weeks.

"What was that all about?" I asked Katie when we returned to our table.

"Gus is always getting into trouble," Katie said. "And he's always blaming his troubles on other people. He even tried to blame Esme when she was still alive."

"Esme?"

Katie shook her head. "He accused her of multiple instances of witchcraft. He makes those in Salem look like sweet, worried old men."

"Did she—uh—do anything to him?"

"Of course not. Esme would have never used her powers for evil. She was the Grand Witch, after all. But he claimed she did. Every time he broke the law—which was a lot—he said she made him do it. No one in town wants him here, but Jake feels an obligation to keep an eye on him. He won't let him leave."

"Why?" I asked.

"Jake feels partially responsible for him. He used to date Gus's daughter, and Gus took him under his wing as a son."

"I bet Gus wasn't thrilled when Jake dated my mother."

"He practically went out of his mind when he found out. That's what put him in jail the first time."

"What did he do?"

"He did many things that never actually ended in proper punishment. But when Jake started dating Emily, Gus vandalized Jake's truck and Jake's parents' house with spray paint. Jake tried to talk his father out of pressing charges, but his father had enough of Gus's antics. Gus got the maximum penalty. Probably because no one wanted to deal with him anymore."

"When did he get out of jail?" I asked.

"He only spent about a year in there the first time, but then he started doing worse and worse things. This last stint was his longest. Five years, I think. He got out about a month ago. I'm surprised it took him this long to make his presence known."

Bex walked out of the kitchen and set our plates of

steaming food on the table. "Was that Gus out here making all that racket?"

"Him and Marty," Katie said.

"I hope he doesn't do anything stupid this time." Bex shook her head. "The last time he was out, he tried to destroy the entire square. Broke out all the windows and even cut down one of the gigantic trees."

"The oldest tree in town," Katie said. "He's a menace. He thinks aliens are coming. He was trying to warn us."

"But then a guy named Marty came in defending the aliens," I said.

"Marty, as in Marty Jafferty?" Bex said.

"Yeah, why?" Katie asked.

"Marty was one of the business owners whose business didn't make it after Gus's rampage."

"That's right," Katie said. "How could I have forgotten Marty's Meats?"

"His meats were forgettable, that's how," Bex said.

"Something no guy wants to hear," Katie joked.

"Oh my gosh, that's gross," Bex said through laughter. I couldn't help but laugh, too.

"Do you think they'll be okay figuring things out on their own?" I asked when we'd all settled down from Katie's joke.

"No," Bex said. "But they're grown adults. No one should feel the need to mediate for them."

Katie nodded. "Agreed."

I took a bite of the sandwich and closed my eyes to savor it. "This is delicious."

"I'll let the Charlies know," Bex said as she headed into the kitchen.

"Do you think there are really aliens?" Katie asked.

"Five years ago, I didn't know there were witches," I said. "Maybe aliens aren't as far-fetched as they seem."

5

Walking into my house with a full stomach and my sweet Penelope trotting up to greet me made me smile. It was good to be home.

I'd neglected my therapeutic recreation business for so long. I didn't even want to check how many missed emails I'd gotten from people trying to book appointments. Thankfully, I'd had enough sense to block off the time. The last thing I needed was to have people showing up at my studio or expecting me at their homes.

"I need to do it and get it over with," I said to Penelope, who oinked beside me. "Maybe I should get a computer to deal with all this. This new phone is great, but a computer would probably make this easier."

I started the coffee maker—I'd need all the energy I could get to deal with the massive number hovering over my mail app icon in the tiny red bubble. Surely not all of those would be requests for my services. There had to be some junk mail in there, too.

By the time I'd weeded through the massive list, the coffee pot was empty, and only eight emails needed replies.

One name caught my eye—Marty Jafferty.

I tapped the message with the subject line: Whole Body Adjustment

Hi. My body hurts and Hank said you could help. I was in a fight with my neighbor and he pushed me down his concrete stairs. Now I can't move at all.

The message was signed with Marty's name and phone number. The date of the email was only a couple of days ago—while I'd been in Colorado.

He didn't look too sore tonight when he'd picked a fight with Gus, but who was I to judge? The only thing I knew was that this guy seemed good at getting into fights.

I replied with several options, double-checked that I'd successfully opened appointment slots, rinsed my coffee cup, and headed to bed with Penelope on my heels.

Before the sun rose, my phone rang with Jake's face on the screen. I hadn't even programmed it to do that yet. Smartphones were so smart.

"Hello?"

"Good morning, Sunshine," he said, his voice not matching the joy of his words.

"You sound like it might not be such a good morning," I said. "What's going on?"

"You'll never believe this, but—"

"Did aliens abduct someone last night?" I laughed. I'd dreamt about aliens all night. In one dream, they were even stealing Penelope in their flying saucer beam.

"Uh, well, that's possible," Jake said. "We have a case of crop circles, a missing man, and a dead man."

I gasped. "I was kidding. Who's missing? Who's dead?"

"Gus is missing, and Marty is dead." Jake sighed. "A couple of people said you were at the café last night when they came in fighting?"

I told him an abbreviated version of the story while I put on some clothes and smoothed my hair into a ponytail. "But doesn't Gus have an ankle tracker thing?"

"It says he's in his house, but so far, we haven't found the tracker or Gus," Jake said. "From what you've told me, it sounds like Gus tried to warn the town."

"He didn't say anything about someone ending up dead," I said. "Just probed and abducted."

"Could you come to the crime scene and give me a hand? I'm at Gus's house—a few miles down your road to the west."

"Already on my way," I said, picking up Penelope and heading down the stairs.

"Also, could you talk to Renée about the possibility of the crop circles being magic related? Maybe someone with questionable magic created them to make it look like aliens."

I hadn't even considered that. "I can do that."

"Thanks," Jake said. "I'll see you soon."

We hung up, and I tried to call Renée, but her phone went straight to voicemail. I left a message about what was happening and then hurried to the garage. As I was pulling out in Mona, I slammed on the brakes.

My field wasn't corn this year—it was soybeans—but at least a hundred tents and their inhabitants were completely trampling those beans.

"What in the heck?" I turned Mona off and hopped out. Penelope had already gotten out and was running around the field, squealing.

People started emerging from the tents, dressed in all sorts of strange things. It took me a minute to realize every single person wore something related to aliens. Some were dressed in bright green, full-body leotards with antennae on their heads, while others simply wore pajamas with cute little aliens on them.

"What is going on?" I mumbled, then walked to the nearest person and asked again. "What is going on?"

"We appreciate your hospitality," said the woman wearing a fluffy green one-piece costume. "I'm sure the others will appreciate your willingness to accommodate us as well."

"The others?" I asked, but she'd moved on with no additional explanation.

I picked up the phone and tapped on Jake's contact. "Hello?"

"Hey, sorry to bug you," I said. "But I have—well—I don't know what I have over here."

"I need you to be more specific. Are you in danger?"

"No," I blurted. "I don't think so. But there are a bunch of people camping in my soybean field. I think they're alien enthusiasts."

"Did they say something about the field? Or Gus? Or Marty?"

"I only talked to one of them, who just thanked me for accommodating them."

"I'll come over and chat with them. Then I can bring you here. Does that work?"

"Sounds good," I said. "I'll be in the barn. I need to clean up a bit, anyway."

We hung up, and I hurried to the barn, trying not to attract any attention from the other squatters. Penelope trotted along after me and squeezed inside as the door was about to close.

This plan worked well, anyway. I needed to get the studio in tip-top shape since clients would be coming again. It had gotten dusty since I'd not used it in weeks.

My phone vibrated in my pocket when I was halfway finished with the floor.

Renée's face popped up on the screen.

"Hello?" I said.

"I got your message," Renée said. "I can't come right now—I'm working on something important—but you can try to detect magic as well, if not better than I can. Look for it like you would with anything else."

"Okay, I'll do that," I said.

We hung up, and I started sweeping again when the

corner of my mother's mural on the back wall caught my gaze. The curtain had been pulled almost all the way closed, but some of it was exposed.

And it wasn't the scene it had been before I'd gone to Colorado.

6

I dragged the curtain back, revealing a mural so stunning it took my breath away. Maybe it was because it hadn't changed for a while, or maybe it was the vivid colors and detail. Either way, it was different.

The angle was from the far side of the field, looking toward the back of the barn and the house. The magical pond was in the distance between the painter and the house. Little heads floated in the pond as if the entire town had come for a party. Not that that was possible since most of the town didn't possess magical abilities and had no idea the pond was even back there.

But the most intriguing part was the field. Or, rather, what hovered above the field. A circular spaceship with a triangular beam of light widening as it reached from the ship to the ground was the main focal point of the mural. In the middle of the beam—as if being lifted into the air— was a figure of a person.

I took a step closer to inspect.

The person was unrecognizable.

The barn door opened as I reached up to touch the light beam.

"Ellie? Are you in here?" Jake's voice wafted from the studio.

I desperately wanted to look at the painting more—especially for any sparks of magic that might explain the mural's message. But I couldn't do that with Jake present.

"I'm over here," I said, dropping my arm and stepping back.

Jake walked past the curtain.

"Did you find Gus?" I asked.

Jake shook his head. "Not yet. Have you heard from Renée?"

"She told me to look for any magical traces."

"Sounds good." His gaze was fixed on the mural. "When did this happen?"

"I just found it this way," I said.

"Interesting timing," Jake said. "I think I know why alien people are in your field."

He held up his phone to show me a picture of my mailbox and a massive plywood sign with a spray paint message leaned up against it.

Friends of the Others Welcome

"That's it?" I asked. "They're all squatting here because of a welcome sign?"

"We have some of our tech guys searching their servers, but I would guess whoever put up the sign also sent out a message that your field was available for camping."

I groaned.

"Do you want me to tell them they have to leave?" Jake asked. "You have every right to kick them off your property."

"Except someone might know something about the case," I said.

Jake nodded.

"Then let them stay for now. They can't do any more damage than has already been done."

"Are you sure?"

"Yeah," I said. "And while I'm thinking about it, I got a message from Marty a couple of days ago about coming in for a session. I'd been on hiatus, but it might give us somewhere to start. He said he'd fought with one of his neighbors."

I opened the email and handed him the phone.

Jake groaned. "Can you send this to me?"

"Sure," I said, and as I did, I asked. "Why the groan?"

"Marty's only neighbor is Gus."

I put Penelope in the house before Jake and I made our way down the dusty country road to Gus's property.

As we drove, the sun rose, warming the cool autumn day.

"Good to see you, Ellie," Deb—Jake's partner—said

when we arrived. She always looked serious and professional in her uniform. Very different from her younger sister, Bex, who was more of a free spirit.

"Nice to see you too," I said.

"Give us the rundown?" Jake asked.

"As you can see, the cornfield was—uh—circled? I don't know the correct verb for creating crop circles. But circles were created by the downed stalks of corn."

We stepped through the field. Rows and rows of cornstalks had been pushed down—not cut—in a pattern of massive circles. Just like mine at home.

"Do you really think it was aliens?" I asked.

"If it wasn't magic, I can't think of a better explanation," Jake said.

Deb and Jake watched me expectantly.

I hadn't seen anything even slightly magical since I'd arrived at Gus's house, but I checked again more closely.

As my gaze swept the field, I only saw a lost crop and a crime scene. No magic whatsoever.

I shook my head. "I don't see any magic."

This seemed to be enough confirmation for them.

"But I also don't know that it was aliens," I said. "This could be some sort of hoax."

"Pretty big hoax," Jake said. "I can't imagine what it would take to do this to all of this in one night without anyone noticing."

Deb and I exchanged glances. I assumed we were both thinking the same thing.

"Do you think it could actually be aliens?" I finally asked.

"I think it's just as possible that it was aliens as it could have been magic or a hoax."

I didn't meet Deb's eye for fear that we'd start laughing. Not that I was the expert on strange phenomena because, well, my hair changed color and shape with my moods for twenty-some years, and I never considered it was due to my being a witch.

"What kind of evidence did you find near Marty?" I asked. "Any cause of death?"

"Neve hasn't arrived yet," Jake said, checking his watch. "I would have expected her by now."

Little did he know Neve was driving back from Colorado as we spoke. She'd driven out to help me with the case. She was a witch, but no one knew that. No one but me.

"We'll process the scene without her, and she can do her evaluation in the morgue," Deb said.

"Marty lived next door?" I asked. "Maybe he came here to pick another fight with Gus."

"Another fight?" Deb asked.

Jake showed her the email I'd forwarded to him.

She handed him his phone.

"What made you come to Gus's house in the first place?" I asked.

"We got an anonymous call from someone on the alien website," Deb said. "They told us they saw a video of an alien encounter. We haven't gotten the video yet, but we noticed Gus's field was flattened when we looked for the encounter. Then we found Marty's body."

"Have you been able to trace the call? Maybe whoever called is who did it?"

"Untraceable," Jake said. "It was too quick, and we think it came from a burner phone."

"Before we head into the field," Deb said, "I think we should start in the house."

The house looked like a tornado had ripped through it without removing the doors or the roof. "Is this the way Gus's house typically looks?" I asked, trying to step over the papers and tchotchkes littering the floor.

"Couldn't say," Jake said.

"Does he have a wife or children?" I asked.

Deb glanced at Jake.

"Jasmine," Jake said. "We used to date."

I'd forgotten that Katie already told me that.

"Would she know how he lived? Or if anything's missing?" I asked, looking around. "Maybe someone knew Gus was terrified of aliens and used this as a distraction for either killing or robbing him."

"Or maybe he set it up himself to get away with murder and away from Cliff Haven," Deb said.

Jake shook his head. "Gus wouldn't have done that. I know he didn't like it here, but he wouldn't have gone to these extremes."

"Sometimes when a person is in a corner, their only way out is to go to an extreme," Deb said.

"We need to talk to Jasmine. Maybe she can tell if anything's missing," I said. "This could have been a robbery gone wrong."

"She hasn't been to Cliff Haven in years," Jake said. "I

can't imagine—"

"You can't imagine what, Jacob?" a woman in a tight blood-red dress with matching heels and long straight, shiny brown hair said.

Jake cleared his throat as he turned around. "Hello, Jasmine."

"I'd say it's nice to see you, but that would be a lie." Jasmine's voice was quiet but powerful.

"Jasmine, this is Ellie. And you know Deb," Jake said.

"Nice to meet you," I said, holding a hand out for her to shake. I expected her to have a wimpy handshake, but she gripped my hand with strength and authority. So much so I could feel the guilt ripping through her veins.

"Do you work for CHPD?" Jasmine asked, ignoring Deb's outstretched hand.

"I'm not an officer," I said. "Just a consultant."

"You look familiar." She squinted at me. "Have we met? In a courtroom, perhaps?"

"Jasmine is a big wig Chicago attorney," Deb said.

Jasmine turned her narrowed gaze on Deb. "Couldn't leave that out, could we? What did I ever do to make everyone in this town hate me?"

"It's what you didn't do," Jake said. "You couldn't be bothered to show up for your own father."

"Gus doesn't deserve my help," she said. "Not that he would have taken it even if I'd have offered."

"When did you get to town?" I asked, trying to avoid the oncoming argument train threatening to crash in Gus's living room. Though, it wouldn't have made much of a difference in the place.

"Katie called me when Gus was released from jail."

"Wasn't that weeks ago?" I asked.

"It took me a while to get down here." She brushed her silky hair over her shoulder.

"It's interesting timing that you'd show up right after he'd gone missing."

"You don't think I helped him go missing?" She laughed. "That's preposterous." Her inquisitive attorney gaze shifted from me to Jake to Deb and back to me. "Oh. You think I *made* him go missing."

"Where were you last night?" Jake asked.

"Come on, Jake. You didn't think I'd cooperate that easily, did you?" She shook her head with a smile.

"If you don't want to answer that, would you tell us if you think anything is missing in the house?" Jake asked. "Or would anyone have a reason to come into your father's house?"

"Was the entry forced?" Jasmine asked.

Jake smirked. "I can't give you details about the case."

I noticed no signs of forced entry, but I could have missed them.

"Well, if there had been, then I'd guess someone was either here to abduct Gus or here to steal something. Or Gus did it to make it look like that's what happened." She sighed. "Though I don't think he's smart enough or strong enough to make it look like he was robbed or abducted. And it's unlikely that he'd be abducted at all. He's not exactly the type of person someone would want to abduct."

"You don't seem to have a very good relationship with your father," I said.

"Bravo, you should be an investigator," Jasmine deadpanned. "Now, I have some things to gather, if you don't mind."

"This is a crime scene," Jake said.

"Is it?" Jasmine asked. "Maybe this is the way Gus lived. Maybe he came home drunk and destroyed the place. How can you be certain?"

She was good. Confident. I wouldn't want to go up against her in a courtroom.

We all waited to see how Jake would reply.

When he didn't say anything, Deb piped up, "It is a crime scene. Nothing comes in or goes out."

"I'll have a word with the judge about that," Jasmine said. "You better have all your ducks in a row."

"There's a dead body in the cornfield," I said. "I may not be an attorney or an investigator, but with the look of this place, I'd say they could be connected. But sure, go to the judge if your high-profile schedule allows for such menial work."

Jasmine gaped at me, then turned to Jake and said, "Let me know when the crime scene is clear so I can gather some things."

Jake nodded, and Jasmine stormed away.

"Holy moly," Deb squealed. "I can't believe you just said that."

"I couldn't let her bully us," I said. "My guess is she uses her stature and beauty to get what she wants more often than the actual law."

"Be careful with her," Deb said. "She puts on a good face, but she's a lot more like Gus than she'd ever admit. In fact, she's the one who got Gus to believe in aliens in the first place."

7

When we were finished searching through the house, Jake and Deb led me out to the middle of the cornfield, where a swarm of officers dealt with the crime scene.

"Jake, there's something I want you to see," an officer said when she saw us walk up. "We need to consider the alien theory regarding the crop circles."

The officer held her phone out for Jake to look at. I averted my eyes to give him his privacy.

"You should see it too, Ellie," the officer said.

Deb and I looked over his shoulder to see what a glitchy time-lapse video of Gus's cornfield being imprinted with the circles.

"Who's doing it?" Jake asked.

"That's the thing," the officer said. "No one. It's spontaneously happening."

"The video looks like it could be drone footage," I said. "Does anyone around here own a drone?"

"It's not something we police," Jake said. "The FAA is the authority in the airspace."

"Maybe they know if someone owns a drone in the area?" I asked.

"It's worth a shot," Jake said, returning the phone. "Where did you get this footage?"

"It's all over the internet," the officer said.

Jake groaned. "We need to prep for the media."

"And the crazies," Deb said.

"What can I do?" I asked.

"You can do what you always do." Jake gave me a small smile. "You can help us figure out what happened to Marty and Gus and what is happening in this video. There has to be a logical—or otherworldly—explanation."

"Anything new with the scene?" Deb asked.

"No blood, seemingly no injuries—though we haven't turned him over—and no sign that anyone brought the body out here. It's almost like he was dropped from the sky," an officer said.

"After the crop circles were made, right?" I asked. "Otherwise, his body would be beneath the stalks."

"Can we tell how long he's been dead?" Deb asked.

"Not without Neve," the officer said. "Is she almost here?"

"We'll take the body to the morgue, and she can do the autopsy there," Deb said. "Make sure you have excellent pictures of the scene."

Jake got a phone call and excused himself.

"I'm heading home," I said. "Speaking of crazies, I have a bunch camped out in my field."

"Jake told me when you were on the phone," Deb said. "Do you need a ride?"

"Nah, it's okay," I said. "I wore my running shoes. It'll be a good excuse to exercise this morning."

"Be careful. There could be a murderer or a kidnapper on the loose," Deb said.

"Isn't there always?" I laughed as Deb gaped at me in horror. "Kidding. Just kidding."

I totally wasn't kidding.

The police were still examining the field as I jogged toward my house.

On foot, seeing all the damage done to Gus's field was much easier. The farmers were probably in a tizzy about it. What if it happened to one of theirs next?

I knew what I had to do first—go to Katie's Café. If anyone knew anything about what happened last night, they'd be at the café.

When I jogged into my driveway, I hopped in Mona, who I'd left half in and half out of the garage.

"Sorry I took off like that," I said, glancing at the tents. "Looks like everyone's still here from last night. Do they sleep in the day and wake at night?"

Mona's steering wheel warmed beneath my hands. I'd been told that my magic powered Mona's magic, but I didn't believe it. She had a magic of her own—a powerful and wonderful magic.

I expected the café to be busy, but holy wow, was it busy. Like line out the door busy. It was as if the Trot 'n Tater and the Strawberry Festival were happening on the same day.

The people lined up were dressed like those staying in my field. Apparently, they didn't sleep all day.

I parked Mona in the alleyway and walked in through the alley door to the kitchen.

"What's going on?" I asked.

"Thank goodness you're here," Bex said. "Can you grab some tables for me?"

"Where's Katie?"

"She's out there too," Bex said. "We're full to the gills. Somehow, the alien nuts already heard about the crop circles and are here in droves."

"Just the crop circles?" I asked.

"For the love of all things good in this world, please don't tell me you found another body."

"Okay, I won't tell you," I said. "But I'm surprised you haven't heard."

"The locals took one look at that line and went home," Bex said. "I haven't seen hide nor hair of a single Cliffer that isn't on staff today. Who died?"

The locals called their fellow Cliff Haven residents Cliffers. It used to make me chuckle, but it had grown on me. "Marty Jafferty."

"As in the Marty that was fighting with Gus last night?"

"I believe so," I said. "And they found him in Gus's field."

"What does Gus have to say about it?"

"Gus is missing."

"Oh heavens," Bex said. "How is this always happening?"

One of the Charlies rang the bell. "Order up, Bex."

"Be right there," she said. "Quick, tell me, what happened to Marty?"

"No clue," I said. "But there's a viral video showing the crop circles being made without anyone around."

"No wonder we have all the crazies. Do you think one of them did something to Gus?"

"It's entirely possible," I said, considering this. Maybe they abducted Gus to make it look like aliens. That still didn't explain the crop circles, though. Or the dead Marty.

Bex hurried over to pick up the order.

"Grab an apron and help a girl out." She motioned to the dining room.

It wasn't what I had planned for the day, but if she needed help, I couldn't charge out the door without lending a hand. That wasn't my style.

I grabbed my black half-apron and hurried out.

"Oh, good. I'm glad Bex called you," Katie said, stopping me. "Can you get the three booths up front? They need drinks and orders taken."

"Will do," I said, not bothering to correct her. "How's Earl and the others with this corn fiasco?"

"About how you'd expect," she said. "They're freaking out, worried it could happen to us. Whoever did it—and I know it's not aliens, regardless of what they think—should be prosecuted to the fullest extent of the law. I'd suspect one of them did it to make it look like aliens are real."

I glanced at the dining room, which looked more like an alien costume party than a café.

Trying not to stare, I hurried by a table of women in tight green leotards that extended to their fingers and toes, making them look like their skin was green. Their faces were also painted green, and a couple had antennas on their heads.

The front booth—made for four—was stuffed with six impatient-looking men and women. Two of them wore green leotards, one wore a silver robot-looking costume, and the other three wore costumes that were a mixture of a butterfly and a bear. They had wings they'd gotten into the booth without being too crushed, long claws on the tips of their fingers, and when they spoke to tell me their orders, I had to listen extra carefully to figure out what they were saying between their massive fake teeth.

As I finished taking their order, a person yelled from a table I was supposed to take care of. "Let's get this show on the road. I haven't even gotten my drinks. We don't have all day."

I took a breath, ready to say something in a calm, stern voice when a man stood from the table in the center.

He was a beast of a man standing at around six foot eight, likely weighing as much as a grizzly—at least a female grizzly. I hadn't noticed him before since people surrounded him, but he wasn't dressed like the others. He wore jeans and a cream-colored sweater with the sleeves pushed up to his elbows, exposing his hairy arms.

When he spoke, the entire room quieted. "These people are doing their best. The others know we are here. They have beckoned us. They will not leave without making contact."

I was about to say something when the entire restaurant, minus the staff, said, "Yes, Grandmaster," in unison.

8

By the time we closed the doors that night, it was almost eleven o'clock and completely dark outside. I'd made no progress on the case, but at least the alien followers tipped well.

The man they'd called Grandmaster had left after eating breakfast, but Bex and I had laughed about the whole scene for hours.

As I walked out the back to Mona, I nearly screamed when a dark figure appeared from down the alley.

"It's just me," Xander said. "What is going on in this town?"

"Aliens," I said as if that one word was enough to answer his question.

I hadn't expected to feel awkward around him, but after our whirlwind romantic moments a few days ago and my abrupt return to Cliff Haven, it felt strange to be in his presence. "How's your dad?"

"Stubborn," Xander said, kicking a tiny pebble on the sidewalk. "He refuses to be healed."

"That's too bad," I said. "I'd hoped he would have accepted it. Did you tell him no strings attached?"

"I tried several times, but he's set on letting nature take its course."

I pushed away the fear of rejection sitting in the middle of my chest and slipped my arms around Xander's waist. "I'm sorry. Do you think it would be more effective if I talked to him? Or maybe your mom?"

"Mom tried," Xander said, his voice deep with emotion. "But she eventually gave up. She said if that's what he wants, then that's what he wants."

We stood there in our embrace for what could have been minutes or hours.

When his phone rang in his pocket, he groaned before answering it. "This is Xander." His expression changed from irritation to sweetness in an instant. "Hey, what's going on?"

I wasn't a naturally jealous person, but the high-pitched voice was definitely that of another woman. Between that and his demeanor change, I was interested in who it was.

He let the woman on the other end talk while he mumbled a series of uh-huhs and yeahs.

"I'll talk to him and see what he thinks," Xander said. "It shouldn't be a problem, but I'd like to make sure."

The woman said something else, and they disconnected the call.

"That was Lulu—er—Emily," Xander said. "She wants Eloise to meet Gerald before he dies."

"Makes sense," I said. "When do you expect that to happen?"

"Soon," Xander said. "It has to happen soon. Or it might be too late. Do you want to be there too?"

I considered it for a moment, then shook my head. "No, it's not my place. This is between the four of you and your mom. How do you think she'll take it?"

"If I had to guess, Mom's probably known for ages. She has that mom magic that practically gives her eyes in the back of her head."

He lowered his lips to mine and kissed me so gently it felt like a butterfly landing on my lips. Or maybe a lightning bug. I didn't know if I'd ever get used to the electricity that passed between us when we touched. In fact, I hoped I never did. It was amazing.

"I have to get back," Xander said.

"If you need me to talk to him again, let me know," I said. "I can be there in literal seconds."

He smiled and kissed me one more time before opening Mona's door, then walking back down the alley into the dark.

My entire drive home, I thought about Eloise meeting Gerald. Would she be happy to know him even if she had little time to spend with him? Would Gerald accept her as his daughter?

Pulling into the driveway to see all the tents still caught me slightly off guard.

I parked Mona in the garage and locked the door. The last thing I needed was someone breaking in and trying to take her. Though, they'd probably end up on the losing side of that transaction. Mona was a scrappy lady.

Thankfully, Penelope had stayed locked in the house and couldn't leave through the piggy door.

As I approached the tents, I could hear Penelope's squeals inside the house. She was probably itching to get out here and check it out again.

I stopped in my tracks. Jake would kill me if I didn't tell him I was about to talk to them, and then something happened to me.

I sent him a quick text.

When I looked up from my phone, a man had emerged from a big tent. The Grandmaster from the restaurant. I did my best not to laugh, thinking of one of Bex's many jokes.

"Can I help you?" he asked as if this wasn't my property he and his followers were squatting on.

I took a deep breath and focused on my magic, especially not letting my hair change color. I had no idea what these people would do if they met an alien, let alone a witch. "I was going to ask you the same thing. This is my field."

He looked me up and down. "You don't look like the owner of this field."

"Why? Because I'm young? A woman? Blonde?"

"Because you're human," he said as if that was the most obvious thing in the entire world. "This field belongs to the others now. They've marked it as theirs."

"The others? As in the aliens? And how have they marked it?"

He frowned. "They don't much like to be called aliens."

"And you would know that how?"

"I've spoken with them," he said, keeping his voice calm. "They chose me to be the leader of their human cohort on Earth."

"Why would they need a human cohort?"

"They're not so boastful as to think they're the superior lifeforms, though I would argue they are. They think they can learn from humans."

"And what do they think about being the prime suspects in a murder case?" I asked.

The Grandmaster gasped. "They would never harm a human."

"Really? Because we found a dead one in the middle of their work of art. I'm sure you noticed the police cars and tape when you went by."

"Someone could have taken the body out there to frame the others." He spoke about them as if they were his best friends. "They're not dangerous. They don't kill like we do."

"Do you have any idea who might want to frame them?"

"The unbelievers," he answered without a single second of thought. "It has to be."

"And who exactly are these unbelievers?" I asked. "Is it anyone who doesn't believe in them or a specific group?"

"The unbelievers are a very specific group," the Grandmaster said. "You'll know them by the rings they wear."

I wanted to throw my hands in the air and go inside to

be with Penelope, but the thing about the rings stopped me. "What do the rings look like?"

"They claim to be a farmer's society, but it's a cover for the humans against the others coming to earth. Why else would the others attack the cornfields?"

I was afraid he would say something like that. I'd seen several of the farmers around town wearing gold rings engraved with three-pronged tridents.

"And these are your followers?" I waved my hands around at the other tents. I didn't want to get him more riled up about my farmer friends.

"These are not my followers," he said. "They're followers of the others. And don't even think about trying to kick us out of here. If you do, the others will punish you."

"Haven't I already been punished?" I asked. "I'm not part of this farmer group you speak of, and yet my field has been just as damaged as Gus's."

"Of course, you're not part of the society. You're a woman. And a witch."

I sucked in a breath, ready to tell him how that surely was incorrect, when the flashing lights of a police car came pulling into the driveway.

"You called the police?" The Grandmaster gaped at me. "Maybe I was wrong. Maybe you are part of the society."

I was usually a very patient person, but this guy was getting on my last nerve.

Esme's words came back into my mind—kill him with kindness. I plastered a smile on my face.

Jake stepped out of his police car and walked toward us casually, but he looked worried. He'd probably sent me a message telling me not to engage. Though, I'd think he'd know me better than that by now.

"I thought we already spoke about this, Mr. Hagley," Jake said. "You were supposed to get everyone off Ellie's property today. There is a campground up the road at the state park."

"Please, call me Gorvich or Grandmaster. The others don't want us to be in the state park. They want us here, ready for them. That's why they sent us these signals."

"The others did not create that sign against Ellie's mailbox."

"Well, we couldn't camp where we were supposed to—in the circled field," Gorvich said, raising his hands.

"Because it's the scene of a murder," Jake said.

"Maybe if these farmers hadn't actively plotted against the others, the others would have left their property alone."

"I'd like to see the others try to do the same thing to any of the remaining farms. The farmers are ready and on guard."

"That's exactly why they'll be punished, and she will be rewarded."

"I don't think Ellie is looking to support the others," Jake said. "Now, if you could please—"

"You know what?" I said, interrupting Jake. "They can stay. I'd love to be on good terms with the others."

Gorvich's face widened into a smile. "Looks like I was wrong about you. The others and I thank you for your cooperation." He turned and walked to his tent without another word.

"Why did you give in to his request?" Jake asked.

"Because I still think he could help us with the case," I said. "Especially if someone from his cohort had something to do with all this."

"You think one of these people could have killed Marty?"

"Sometimes, when you want something badly enough to be true, you make it true."

Something in my mind clicked into place. What if thinking it was impossible to cure my mother without Gerald's help made it impossible? Could we change our mindsets and heal her without Gerald's magic?

"What's that look on your face?" Jake asked.

"Nothing," I said too quickly.

"Hmmm . . . doesn't look like nothing."

I couldn't tell him about Emily. He'd want to see her, and that could ruin everything. There was no way I would let him explode her brain just because he was in love with her.

Or was he?

He had Georgia now.

Maybe I could tell him, and he would shrug it off.

"Earth to Ellie," he said. "You doing okay, or did the aliens suck out your brain and give you a new name like our friend Gorvich?"

"Wait, Gorvich isn't his real name?"

"Nope," Jake said. "His real name is George Hagley. But he says after his encounter with the others, he was renamed Gorvich, though he still goes by George in his business."

"Interesting," I said. "Has anyone else claimed to have an encounter with the others?"

"Not that I'm aware of," Jake said. "But we haven't spent much time talking to them. Between the murder case and the unexpected influx of people, we're maxed out."

"Influx of people?"

"This is only one cohort of alien followers," Jake said. "Somehow, this cohort heard about the circles before all the others. Probably had an inside source. More people believe in this stuff than you'd think. I'd venture to guess at least one Cliffer is part of their online cohort."

"Can you do some digging and find out who?"

"Do you think it could be related to the case?" Jake asked.

"It feels too coincidental that the day before these crop circles were made, Gus was going around town warning us that the aliens were coming. Then he ends up missing, and Marty ends up dead in his ruined field. Maybe he crossed the wrong alien cohort member."

"Interesting thought," Jake said. "If you think you can talk to some of them carefully, go for it. Maybe in the morning when the sun is up."

"Sounds good," I said. "Any word on Gus's whereabouts?"

"No," Jake said. "But when we find him, I'll tell you immediately."

He walked me to my door, where Penelope practically threw herself at my feet.

"Looks like she was worried about you, too," Jake said. "Don't you have a guardian who is supposed to follow you around?"

"She had some business to attend to," I said. "But my

house protects me, Mona protects me, Penelope protects me, you protect me, and basically the entire town protects me. She seems to think I'm covered."

"You're definitely covered," Jake said, wrapping an arm around my shoulder, squeezing me to his side.

I smiled. "Thanks for looking out for me."

"It's what faux-fathers do for their non-daughters."

9

Penelope was on the alert all night. Every time I moved, her head jolted up, and she'd squeal.

Needless to say, I was exhausted by the time morning came. I made my coffee extra strong and took it to the front porch to enjoy the sunrise.

The tents were still in the field, but a few people were wandering around aimlessly. The barn was locked. I wasn't worried about anyone getting in.

One woman caught my eye and hurried over to me. "Do you have any more coffee? I'm dying for a cup."

She wore green onesie pajamas with a hood that went completely over her head and face. Her human eyes were replaced with big black alien eyes created with a mesh material so she could see in front of her.

"You know what? I have a better idea," I said. "If you can wait a bit, I think I can make something happen."

Three phone calls and twenty minutes later, my kitchen was full of women and food.

"How much should we charge?" Nancy asked as she

whipped up another dozen scrambled eggs. She wore red bike shorts and a red tank top with her curly white hair in a bun on top of her head.

"Twenty dollars a plate," Katie said. She wore black leggings and a sparkly green sleeveless cape shawl thing.

"Thirty," Amy said.

"Heck, why not charge them fifty?" Fran asked.

Fran and Amy each had on one of Amy's metal band t-shirts, but Fran wore jeans, and Amy wore leggings.

When I'd called and suggested we make food for these squatters to raise money for the local animal shelter, they were only too happy to head over and start cooking.

I'd since made a few gallons of coffee and told the squatters that breakfast would be served within the hour.

Now, I had a line of people waiting at the back door for the food line to open.

I'd never invited this many people into my house, but the house could take care of itself. It had no problem keeping people out of rooms where they didn't belong.

"Let's do twenty," I said. "It'll keep them coming back for more that way. Are we ready?"

Bonnie—who was responsible for dishing up the food on the paper plates—gave me a thumbs up.

I opened the door to the crowd of tired-looking alien chasers. "Who's hungry?"

People were packed into every nook and cranny of my house, eating and talking in excited whispers about how this might be their chance to meet the others.

"Have you ever seen an alien?" I asked a small group while walking around picking up discarded plates.

"We all have," a woman dressed in a hooded tinfoil shirt said. "It's a requirement of being part of our cohort."

Skepticism flowed through me. "How do you prove you've seen an alien? It's not like you all have videos, right?"

"Gorvich tests us," she said.

"He tests you?"

"Shhh, we're not supposed to talk about it," another woman in a t-shirt with an adorable alien on the front said.

"Oh, I was thinking about joining," I lied. "But if you can't tell me, that's okay."

"You've seen an alien?" T-shirt asked, excitement spreading across her face.

"Isn't that a requirement of the group?" I asked.

"What was your experience like?" Tinfoil asked.

"I don't know," I said. "Maybe I should wait to see if you really are the most legit group. I don't want to tell my story to anyone, you know?"

Tinfoil looked at T-shirt pleadingly.

"Okay, we'll tell you about the process," T-shirt said. "Only because we want you in our group if you've seen one."

Tinfoil let out a little squeal, clapping her hands together. "So Gorvich asks you a bunch of questions about what happened, and then you have to drink a truth serum and tell the story all over again. If he thinks you're being honest, he sends you through the other detector to make sure an alien has not taken you over."

"Taken over?"

"Like your mind, or whatever, I guess sometimes aliens will use mind control to infiltrate these groups to find out what we know about them."

"Are aliens dangerous?" I asked. "Gorvich made it sound like they were nice."

"Most are really nice," T-shirt said. "But, like humans, not all aliens are the same."

"Do you think one of them could have hurt the man who died in the cornfield a couple of houses down?"

They looked at each other as if no one wanted to say anything.

"Was he murdered?" T-shirt said. I could tell she already knew the answer to that question by her tone.

"He was," I said. "And it doesn't look like something a human could have done."

I was embellishing a bit. I didn't know that, but the lie might be worth it if it helped me get information from this group.

"He was probably part of that farmer society Gorvich keeps talking about," T-shirt said.

I needed to talk to Katie and Nancy about this. I was pretty sure Earl and Hank wore the rings Gorvich had described.

"Do you know a man by the name of Gus Norton?" I asked.

"Oh sure," Tinfoil said. "He's one of our most outspoken haters."

"He's also missing," I said.

The women looked at each other, doing their best to act surprised. Too bad they weren't talented actresses.

"Do you think it's possible someone in another cohort did something to him?" I asked. "Or maybe the others?"

Not a single person spoke.

"Or maybe the others chose him," I said, trying to get them to say something.

"Unlikely," T-shirt said.

"Why do you think so?" I asked. "Maybe they wanted to change his mind and send him to Earth to relay the message."

"Look, I think the others know we'd all be seriously peeved if they abducted Gus over one of us."

Tinfoil nodded.

I shrugged.

"Didn't you find that body in Gus's cornfield?" T-shirt asked.

"Not me specifically, but yes," I said.

"Maybe Gus murdered him and then took off, leaving the others to get blamed."

Tinfoil nodded harder. "That's probably what happened."

"How did you all find out about the crop circles?" I asked. "You must have some great intel since you beat all the other cohorts here."

"Someone knew," T-shirt said. "Someone knew this was coming."

"Shhh," Tinfoil said. "We're not supposed to discuss this with anyone."

"I won't tell a soul," I said.

T-shirt waited for Tinfoil to give her a nod of approval before she said, "There was someone on our chat server who hasn't been identified. They predicted the circles and abduction but said nothing about the murder."

"Do you think it could have been Gus?" I asked.

They both shook their heads.

"The person posting hates Gus," T-shirt said.

It sounded like this person was someone we needed to find. "Can I see the chats?"

Tinfoil narrowed her eyes at me. "I think we've given you enough information to make your decision. If you want to see the chats, join the cohort." She grabbed the other woman by the arm and dragged her to another side of the living room.

T-shirt mouthed an apology as she was pulled away.

"Oh my gosh," a voice whispered behind me. "I can't believe it."

"Where did you get this?" another person whispered.

I acted like I was collecting plates as I glanced over to see what they were looking at.

Five people surrounded a large laptop, and a video looped repeatedly on the screen.

It seemed to be taken from above Gus's farm—possibly from the roof or a drone—and showed several all-green figures moving through the corn. And as they did, the corn just laid down into the circles. My heart raced.

"I didn't expect the others to have to physically create the circles," one of the people whispered.

"We've never known until now," another said in awe. "They make it look effortless."

I needed to figure out how to get this footage to Jake. I inched closer to see the website's name—There Are Others.

10

I hurried to the kitchen and called Jake.

"There's a new video going around on private chat servers." I gave him all the information I could remember about the site, including the name—There Are Others—and then told him what the women had told me.

"Sounds like we have some new suspects," Jake said. "Thanks for the information. I heard you're raising money for the animal shelter over there. Any chance you have a plate of breakfast left?"

"I think we can make that happen," I said before hanging up.

"What was that all about?" Fran asked.

"There's a video that surfaced on a chat group. It shows what looks like aliens making crop circles."

Amy gasped.

"Katie, Nancy, I have a question for you both."

"Go ahead, sweetie," Nancy said.

"Those rings that Earl, Hank, and some other farmers wear. What are they for?"

"They're for their secret farmer's society," Nancy said. "It's an old tradition. They make farming predictions, discuss what fertilizers to use, and have way more coffee than anyone needs. Why do you ask?"

"Are they anti-alien?" I asked.

Katie chuckled. "What do you mean?"

"Do they have a part of their society that is firmly against aliens?"

Katie and Nancy exchanged a questioning glance.

"I don't think so," Nancy said.

"At least not that I know of," Katie said. "Why do you ask?"

"Some of the cohort members think Gus was part of the society, and that's the reason Marty was found dead in his cornfield."

"That's ridiculous," Nancy said, shaking her head. "I wouldn't put any stock in that theory."

"That's what I thought, but I had to ask." I smiled. "How'd we do with the breakfast?"

"We made five thousand dollars," Fran said. "Some of them had seconds and thirds."

"This was a great idea," Amy said.

"I'm pleasantly surprised by the turnout," I said. "I thought the twenty-dollar price tag might have been too steep."

"Don't judge this group by their looks and tents," Amy said. "I overheard some of them talking. The ones in Gorvich's cohort all seem very well to do."

"You wouldn't know it by the buses they drove and the tents they slept in, but one of them owns the biggest motel chain in the country," Fran added.

This changed my entire viewpoint. I guess I hadn't pictured wealthy businessmen as alien chasers who stayed in crappy tents in the middle of a flattened cornfield.

"Jake will be by soon to grab a plate of food," I said. "I'll take the coffee carafe outside and top a few people off. Maybe I can get some more information while I'm out there."

"Good idea," Nancy said.

I slipped on my shoes. "Penelope, do you want to come with me?"

She oinked and hurried to the door.

"Don't worry about cleaning up," I said. "I can do that when I get back."

"You think we'd leave this mess for you?" Katie laughed. "We got this under control."

"Thank you. For everything."

Penelope and I started into the field when my phone rang.

"Hello?" I answered, knowing it was Jake.

"We found Gus," Jake said. "He was hiding out in his attic. I have an officer taking him down to the station, and I think Neve has some information for us, too."

"I'll be over right away," I said before hanging up. "Looks like I'm going to the police station, Penelope. Let's get you back in the house."

She squealed and tore off toward the magical pond in the backyard.

"Penelope!" I called. "Do not do this. Jake needs my help."

But she didn't stop until she was right at the edge of the pond.

She knew how to swim. I wasn't afraid of her going in. The only thing that worried me was that she hardly ever did this. She was usually great about sticking around. Until recently, that is.

I walked quickly but softly behind her. I didn't want to freak her out.

When I reached the pond's edge, I knew that wouldn't happen. She stared into the center of the water, where my ghostly grandmother seemed to be swimming.

I almost laughed at the sight of her shimmering body gliding through the unnaturally clear and calm water, not causing a single ripple.

"You wanted me to see Esme swimming?" I asked Penelope.

She grunted beside me but didn't take her eyes off the ghost in the pond.

As Esme swam toward us, Penelope's little curly tail wiggled.

"Is this really more important than helping solve a murder?" I asked.

Penelope didn't make any indication that she even heard me.

"Oh my," Esme said when she reached the shore, and Penelope started oinking loudly. "What do we have here?"

She stood up wearing a swim cap and a one-piece swimsuit, though she didn't seem to have retained any water.

"Let me change into something decent," Esme said.

She disappeared briefly, and when she reappeared, she wore a summery shift dress that went down past her knees.

"Penelope wanted me to come out here," I said.

"That's a good little piggy," Esme said before turning her attention to me. "I told her to bring you here."

"You did?" I asked. "Why?"

"You're always running around doing things. It's hard to keep up."

"Things have been kind of busy lately." I waved my hand toward the house. "All these people, and then someone died. Gus—wait—you know or knew Gus, didn't you?"

"If you're talking about Gus Norton, then yes. He was a horrible human being."

"Do you think he could have killed anyone?"

She tapped her chin with her finger dramatically. "I wouldn't put it past him. He never was that type to temper his emotions."

A thought popped into my head. "Do you think the man he might have killed is a ghost? Maybe I could just ask him who did it."

Esme shook her head. "I have no idea. Maybe. I only know from experience, but I don't remember my death."

"You don't?"

"Nope," she said. "Maybe because I was so sick at that point. But no matter how hard I try, I don't remember dying. It's like one day I was lying in my bed—now your bed—and then the next I was floating and coming to terms with the fact that I'd passed on."

"Does everyone become a ghost when they die?" I asked.

"I don't think it's reserved for the magical. But I don't think everyone does. I think I remain as a ghost because I wanted to meet you and see your mother again."

"Speaking of daughters," I said. "I met Gus's daughter, Jasmine."

Esme wrinkled her nose. "How was she? When I knew her, she was horrible."

Penelope oinked loudly as if she agreed with Esme.

"But Jake dated her," I said. "I wouldn't think he'd date someone that bad."

"People change," Esme said. "But even then, Jasmine took him for all he was worth."

"She used him?"

"For more than his money," Esme said. "And not the other thing you're thinking, either. She used him to get out of trouble."

"Now, she's an attorney," I said. "Apparently, a high-profile one."

"Sounds about right," Esme said. "She was smart enough and conniving enough."

"From what I could tell when I met her, she and Gus didn't have a good relationship."

"I wouldn't suspect so," Esme said. "Gus was a horrible father. I suppose he deserves most of the credit for how she turned out."

"If I wanted to reach out and talk to Marty as a ghost, how would I do that?"

"I tried that many times when I was helping Jake. It seemed like the easiest way to figure out who the murderer was. But I never talked to ghosts who didn't approach me first."

Getting Marty's ghost to approach me wasn't impossible, but it was a challenge I wasn't ready to take on at this very moment.

"Before you take off to solve all the world's problems, I wanted to ask you if you saw Emily?"

There was so much to tell her when all I wanted to do was hurry off to the police station. She was my grandmother, though, and she'd been pretty patient waiting for news of her daughter.

"We found her," I said. "But she remembers nothing. She hired Xander's dad to put a spell on her so she would forget everything the moment she dropped me off at the fire station."

Esme gasped.

"There's more." I thought about how to tell her everything quickly and concisely. "She has a daughter named Eloise, whose father is Xander's father—Gerald. Since Gerald created the spell, he has to remove it, but he's currently dying in a hospital bed. He refuses to let me heal him."

Esme clapped a hand over her mouth as tears glistened in her eyes.

"He said if we try to reintroduce her memories, it could make her brain explode—whatever that means." I sucked in a breath. "Either way, it doesn't seem like the right course of action."

"My sweet girl," Esme said, reaching toward me, then dropping her hands as she likely remembered that she couldn't make physical contact with me as a ghost. "How are you handling all this?"

"I'm handling it," I said. "I'm thankful she's alive. And

it was great meeting her, even if she doesn't remember who she is."

"What about Xander? How does he feel?"

"Conflicted. Angry. Sad. Surprised. Shocked." I shook my head. "He and I seem to be a thing now. Don't worry. I made sure his dad wasn't mine as well."

This made Esme chuckle. "That would have been terrible."

"You're telling me! I kissed him!" I laughed with her.

"I wish I could hug you," Esme said when our laughter died. "I'm sorry you have to go through all of this."

"I'm determined to figure out how to fix her memories without exploding her brain. Even if Xander's father refuses to help. Even if he dies."

"I can't believe he'd rather die than be healed and help."

"I even offered to heal him without making him promise to help, but he refused."

She frowned. "I don't know Gerald well, but he never struck me as anything but a scrappy fighter. It's unlike him to give in to death."

I shrugged. "I have no idea. Xander told me he'd call if Gerald changed his mind."

"At least you have the aliens and this case to keep you occupied."

My stomach dropped. "Are you saying aliens are real?"

"I'm not saying that, but I'm not saying they're not either."

11

The police station was small and clean. When I walked in, the woman behind the reception desk buzzed me in without me having to introduce myself. Jake must have told her I'd be heading that way.

I walked down the hallway to Jake's office to find it empty. There were various interrogation rooms and conference rooms, and I wasn't certain which one Jake and Gus would be in. I texted him that I was waiting in his office and sat back in the chair to think.

I assumed the reason Jake brought Gus in was because he suspected Gus of murder.

Maybe Neve's report would help it all make sense. The lack of evidence at the scene was the most suspicious part, in my opinion. But perhaps it meant someone knew exactly what they were doing. Or maybe Marty had gone out in the field and died of natural causes. I hadn't seen a manner of death, after all.

A photo on Jake's desk caught my eye. He and Georgia

looked so happy together. They were dressed up for some function or another, with big smiles as they held each other close.

Guilt fell in the pit of my stomach. Would bringing my mother back be worse for everyone? Was I the only one who would benefit from it?

Emily was happy right now. She had the diner and Eloise. And she and I could be friends. She didn't need to know I was her daughter. Did she?

"Hey," Jake walked in, looking frazzled. "Ready?"

I almost fell out of my chair.

"Are you okay?"

"Yeah, sorry, lost in thought," I said. "Are you?"

"I'm good," Jake said. "It took quite a lot to convince Gus to come out once we realized he was in the attic. I guess I'm just tired."

"I brought you some breakfast," I said, handing him the plate Katie had whipped up for him. "Katie said you could heat it in the microwave for a few seconds to bring it to temperature."

Jake smiled. "That's awesome. I'll have to eat it later, but I'll put it in my mini fridge for safekeeping."

He reached under his desk and slipped the plate into his hidden fridge.

"You ready to work your magic on Gus?"

I raised my eyebrows.

"Not your actual magic," Jake said. "Unless you can do that."

I shook my head. Maybe I could sense things when I touched people, but that wasn't admissible in a court of law.

"Then we'll have to make do with your superb investigation abilities."

"Gus didn't like Esme," I said. "Are you worried he might completely freak out when he sees me?"

"He might not even know you're related. We'll have to wait and see."

Our answer came quickly in the scream that burst from Gus's mouth when I walked through the interrogation room door.

Jake held his hands out in front of him. "It's okay. Ellie is here to help us figure out who killed Marty and left him on your property."

Gus held his handcuffed hands in front of his face, keeping one eye peeking out to watch me.

I mimicked Jake's posture with my hands up, too. "I promise I won't do anything to hurt you."

"Ha! That's a joke!"

I glanced at Jake to see if he wanted me to leave, but he didn't take his gaze off Gus.

"Gus, do you think aliens are responsible for what happened to Marty?" I asked.

Gus's hands lowered slightly. "Of course I do."

"Do you think they're also responsible for the crop circles?" I asked.

Jake slipped into the chair across from Gus, but I held my position by the door. There was no need to frighten him any more than he already was.

"I think they're responsible for everything that's happened," Gus said. "They killed Marty, not me. They might have been trying to kill me, but I got away."

"Did you see the aliens?" Jake asked in practically a whisper.

"I suspect that was the point, wasn't it? Why else would they appear in my cornfield just as Marty and I were having a big fight? When they realized they couldn't take me with them, they framed me for his murder."

"Can you start from the beginning?" Jake asked. "Maybe when you and Marty left the café?"

"Those kids laughed at me. Marty grabbed my underwear. I was trying to do a good thing by warning everyone."

"How did Marty get to your house?" Jake asked.

"He followed me home. I think he was drunk. He was ranting and raving about how I owed him money for his business and how he'd take me to court again if I didn't pay up. I told him he wouldn't get a penny from me. He said he would take my house if that's what he had to do."

"How did you react to that?" Jake asked.

I held my breath. Was he about to confess?

"I wasn't going to kill him if that's what you're getting at," Gus spat. "I was telling him what for when a green light took over the cornfield from above. It caught us both by surprise. Marty was thrilled, of course, since he was one of them believers. Part of some cohort with an alien guy in charge. They were always hassling me about my ring and the farmer society."

"You're part of the farmer society?" Jake asked.

"I was before they kicked me out," Gus said. "They didn't like it much when I went to jail."

"Did the farmer society hate aliens?" I asked.

Gus was startled, as if he'd somehow forgotten I was there. "Who've you been talking to? Don't listen to none of those alien lovers. We weren't haters. Our society was for farming and farming only. There was no need for us to even discuss aliens. They hate us for absolutely no reason."

That was good to know.

"Let's go back to the green light," Jake said, redirecting the conversation. "What happened after that?"

Gus finally seemed to relax, leaning back in his chair. His expression turned contemplative. "Marty walked towards it like he was hypnotized or something. I tried to stop him, but he kept walking. And then I saw the aliens coming from the corn toward him." Gus sat up a bit. "I probably should have gone to him, but I didn't. I ran. And hid."

"Where did you hide?" Jake asked.

"In the attic where you found me."

I couldn't believe what I was hearing. Gus's story sounded like something from a sci-fi movie, not real life. But he seemed sincere, and I couldn't discount the possibility that there was some truth to what he was saying.

"So, you think the aliens killed Marty?" I asked.

Gus nodded. "I didn't see it happen, but I heard something. A strange noise came from outside then the aliens destroyed my house. I didn't have the guts to go out and check. I stayed in the attic.

"But why would the aliens want to kill Marty?" Jake asked, his brow furrowed in confusion. "Especially if he liked them?"

"I don't know. Maybe he was getting too close to the truth. Maybe they thought he was a threat. Or maybe they didn't mean to kill him. All I know is that I had nothing to do with it."

I studied Gus's face carefully, looking for any signs of deception. But his words seemed genuine, and his fear of the aliens was palpable.

Jake stood up, pushing his chair back. "We'll have to investigate this further."

"Can I go?" Gus asked.

"Not yet," Jake said. "We still have evidence that points to you as the prime suspect."

"What evidence? I can explain anything you need me to."

"We'll do everything we can to make the process go smoothly," Jake said.

"You can't keep me here forever," Gus said. "I know my rights."

Jake nodded. "We'll talk again soon."

He ushered me out of the room, letting another officer inside to escort Gus to his holding cell.

"I think we need to investigate this alien theory further," Jake said when we were in the hallway. "Maybe there's some evidence we're not seeing."

I nodded in agreement. "That sounds good. We also need to look into Marty's background and see if there's any reason the aliens might have targeted him specifically. Or if there's any other plausible explanation. Maybe a significant other? Or another enemy?"

"He's single, and Gus was the only one who didn't like him that we can pinpoint. He was a quiet person and kept to himself."

As we walked down the stairs to Neve's office, I

couldn't shake the feeling that there was more to this case than met the eye. And while the idea of aliens seemed far-fetched, I couldn't ignore the possibility that they might be involved. It was up to us to uncover the truth, no matter how bizarre it might be.

Neve looked incredibly professional in her white lab coat. She was a tiny woman with a massive brain. She was also a witch, though no one knew that but me. Somehow, she'd hidden her magic from other witches and warlocks. It would have to mean she was an incredibly powerful witch, but I didn't question it. Keeping it a secret was her prerogative.

"How's it going?" I didn't want to mention that she'd recently been in Colorado helping me with an investigation in case Jake wasn't aware.

"Good for me. Not great for Marty." Neve wrinkled her nose.

"Can you give us the rundown?" Jake asked.

"From the looks of things, he's been dead twenty-four to forty-eight hours," Neve said.

"How did he die?" I asked.

"Not aliens," Neve said with a chuckle.

Neither Jake nor I laughed.

"Wow, tough crowd," Neve said.

"How do you know aliens didn't kill him?" Jake asked.

"Aside from the fact that aliens aren't real," Neve said, eyeing us as if to ask if we agreed with her. "You don't think they're real, do you?"

"I mean, I'm a witch," I said. "And a few years ago, I would have never thought witches were real."

"Witches and aliens are two completely different

things," Neve said. "Plus, I highly doubt an alien would kill someone with a kitchen knife."

"He was stabbed?" I asked.

"Yep," Neve confirmed. "In the back."

"That's brutal," Jake said, shaking his head.

"Any idea who might have done it?" I asked.

"It's looking like Gus might be the culprit," Neve said. "The stab wounds match the knives from Gus's kitchen set—the set that's missing at least one knife, if not two."

"Did any of the knives have blood residue on them, or do we still need to find the murder weapon?" Jake asked.

"None of the knives accounted for from his house have blood remaining on them. Of course, someone could have bleached them, but the fact that the set is missing two suggests the knife used to kill Marty is still out there."

"But where is all the blood?" I asked. "It didn't look like there was blood in the field."

"He was already dead when he arrived in the cornfield, but I did find this." Neve took a pair of tweezers and picked up a tiny red rock from a small pile of rocks on a silver tray. "This is your standard-grade kitty litter. Great for absorption."

"Ah, yes, the good old kitty litter trick," Jake said. "Not so common with your alien murder."

Neve and I both looked at him questioningly.

"I'm kidding," Jake said. "This probably came from Gus's garage. He used the stuff when he worked on cars now and then."

"This was also interesting." She grabbed a small shiny object from the table beside Marty's body. "I found this in Marty's hand. It looks like some kind of device.

I'm not sure what it does yet, but I'll run some tests on it."

Jake and I leaned over to inspect. The device was sleek and silver, with a series of buttons. It seemed to be a remote of some sort.

"Maybe this is alien technology," I said half-jokingly.

Neve chuckled. "Let's not jump to conclusions. It could be anything."

"Can we borrow it for a few minutes?" Jake asked. "Maybe Gus knows what it is."

"How about you snap a picture and take it to him?" Neve offered.

Jake seemed slightly peeved by this suggestion but did it anyway. "Should we go check?"

"Why don't you go check?" Neve said. "I need to chat with Ellie about some—uh—girl stuff."

Jake's face reddened slightly. "Will do. I'll meet you in the lobby when you're done."

"This won't take long," Neve said.

When Jake was gone, Neve's shoulders dropped from around her ears, the tension in the room fading away.

"So? Tell me what happened with your mom," Neve said.

12

I gave Neve the rundown of everything that had happened after she left. Or rather, everything that hadn't happened.

"So he won't let you heal him? He's just going to die and never fix your mom?"

I shrugged. "That's what it looks like. But I'm thinking that maybe we won't need him to fix her. And maybe fixing her is the wrong way to look at it, anyway."

Neve frowned at me. "What do you mean?"

"Maybe I'm being selfish," I said, the weight of the words hanging in the air. "Everyone else is perfectly fine with the way things are. Emily has Eloise and the diner. And I have a new friend. Maybe even two if I can get Eloise to like me."

"If you had a baby and gave up your memory and magic, would you want to stay that way forever?"

I couldn't think that way in an unbiased manner. "Of course, I'd want to know the truth. But that's easy for me to say when I can see both sides. If I didn't know any better? I don't know." The thought that had been sitting in the back of my mind slowly slipped from my lips. "And maybe there was more to Emily wanting to lose her memory. Maybe she wanted to forget Jake and magic and Cliff Haven. Maybe she wanted a normal life free of all that. If I make her remember—give her back her magic— she might have to become the Grand Witch of the States. What if that's one of the main reasons—besides protecting me—that she did what she did? Who am I to think I know what's best for her? Gerald knew what she wanted better than anyone, and he's not budging."

Neve stood in front of me, deep in thought. Finally, she said, "I see where you're coming from. As hard as that must be, I understand what you're saying."

Tears tickled the corners of my eyes. I quickly brushed them away.

Neve opened her arms to hug me.

I happily took her up on her offer.

"You're a better woman—and witch—than I will ever be," she whispered. "Your mom would be proud."

I hugged her for a few more seconds, then pulled away, steadying my breath. "Enough of that. We have a case to solve."

"Text me and let me know if Gus has anything to say about this gadget," Neve said. "It might save me the time trying to figure out what it's for."

I agreed and let myself out.

On my way up the stairs, I wiped the rest of the tears from my eyes and cheeks so Jake wouldn't know I'd been crying.

"Did Gus know what it is?" I asked.

Jake nodded. "He said it was his homemade alien protection."

"Oh," I said, trying not to laugh. "I suppose it didn't work as he'd hoped."

"I mentioned that," Jake said. "And he told me that Marty had wrestled it out of his hands when they saw the green figures in the cornfield."

"It's a good thing he didn't accidentally push the annihilate button," I said. "Unless it was the aliens who stabbed him with the kitchen knife. Then maybe he should have been more wary of the aliens."

"I don't know that any of the buttons would have annihilated the aliens. At least not the way Gus was talking. He made it sound like the device emitted a soundwave that would render the aliens deaf and blind, giving him time to get away if needed."

I laughed. "I was joking about the annihilate button."

"Right," Jake said. "Is everything okay with Neve?"

"She's fine. Just some girl talk." I started toward the door. "Do you think we could take a better look at the crime scene?"

"I think that's a fantastic idea," Jake said.

"Would you mind if I brought Penelope with me?" I asked. "She has some good instincts, and I promise I won't let her get into too much trouble."

"I think we've photographed and taken samples of everything we need. Plus, it's not like we've been able to keep the wild animals out, right?"

I smiled at Jake's comment, happy to have Penelope join us. "She'll be thrilled."

The wind had picked up outside, and the air had

turned chilly. The leaves on the trees rustled and danced in the wind, giving off an eerie sound.

I drove home and picked up Penelope before returning to Gus's house.

When we pulled into the driveway, I first noticed the crime scene tape flying around in various places where the wind had overcome the fastening material. With the corn lying flat, police officers milling about, and television cameras surrounding the field, the place was like a strange mystery movie set.

"Thank God you're here," Jasmine said, stepping out of her fancy electric blue sports car. "Your officers still won't let me in the house."

"They're doing their job," Jake said. "This is a crime scene."

She narrowed her eyes at him. "Don't think you can get your petty revenge on me by stretching out this case."

"I'd like to do everything I can to make sure we find who killed a man, and if that means extra time on a crime scene, then so be it."

I almost patted Jake on the back for standing up to her.

"I need to get into the safe," she said.

"For what purpose?" Jake asked.

"I don't have to tell you that," Jasmine said.

"You're right. You don't." Jake turned and walked in the other direction. Penelope and I followed.

"Ugh, fine," Jasmine said, hurrying after us. "All of Gus's paperwork is in the safe. I need to keep paying his mortgage while he's gone so we don't lose the house."

Penelope let out a low inaudible grumble I could feel against my leg as she leaned up against it.

"This may not look like much compared to your grand-mother's magical mansion," Jasmine said, turning her attention to me, "but this is all I have. I mean, besides my amazing salary and house in the city."

She added the last part so quickly it sounded like a lie. But there was no faking the expensive car she drove. The woman definitely had money.

"I'm sure if you call the bank and explain the circum-stances, they'll let you make a payment," Jake said.

"Okay, it's more than the paperwork," Jasmine said between gritted teeth. "Gus was also holding onto a few things for me that I need."

"He's been out of jail for weeks, and you decide now is the time to pick up your things?" I asked.

"I've been busy," she said.

Jake shook his head. "Once the investigation is over, with Gus's permission, you can get inside. Just stick around town for a bit."

Jasmine blanched at that suggestion.

"It's really not the worst town ever," Jake said. "And your dad isn't the worst dad, either."

"That's easy for you to say. You had great parents," Jasmine spat. "Plus, Gus always loved you like the son he wished he had. Well, until you started dating that witch."

My heart clenched. I hated when people spoke badly of Emily and Esme. "Maybe if you spent your time trying to get your father out of jail instead of trying to get into his house, he'd appreciate you more."

Jasmine turned her head slowly toward me.

We spent the better part of ten seconds staring each other down.

"Look, the crime scene is a crime scene and will be until I say it's not anymore," Jake said, stepping between us.

"I have more important things to do than hang around this awful town," Jasmine said, finally taking her eyes off me and looking at him.

"That's your choice," Jake said before walking away.

I jogged to catch up.

"Maybe she's a suspect," I said when we were out of earshot. "She seems to want this crime scene cleared up as soon as possible, and I doubt it's because of what's in the safe."

"I caught that too," Jake said. "I suspect whatever's in the safe is something she couldn't get to with Gus around."

"Which means if you let her inside, you'd be allowing her to steal from her father."

"Exactly," Jake said. "Which isn't something I want to do."

"Do you think there's any way she might have murdered Marty?" I asked.

"She said she was at work all day and then out at a nightclub when this happened. We're still corroborating her alibi, but if it's accurate, she wouldn't have had time to get from Chicago to Cliff Haven and murder Marty."

"All right," I said. "If it's not her, then we're back to Gus as our prime suspect."

"Now we have to find more evidence that either points to him or someone else," Jake said.

"As long as the wind has blown nothing away," I said.

Penelope oinked up at me in agreement, and the wind stopped almost as if by magic.

"Um, did you do that?" Jake asked, looking at me with wide eyes.

"Nope," I said, then looked down at Penelope. "Did you?"

Penelope oinked again and trotted off toward the cornfield.

I shook my head. "No, there's no way. Penelope isn't magical."

"You sure about that?" Jake asked with a laugh.

I wasn't sure about that, but no one had mentioned anything about animals being magical. Smart, yes. Magical, no.

A whirring noise came from overhead, and Jake and I squinted into the sunny sky to find what looked like a tiny little spaceship with four propellers.

"It's our drone," Jake said. "To get video footage of the farms from above."

"Do you think something is hiding in the corn? Like a message from the aliens or something?"

Jake didn't laugh at my joke. "We need to keep our minds open."

"You think it really could be aliens?" I asked.

"That video seems pretty realistic."

"I mean, maybe. Or maybe someone is really good at video manipulation," I said. "I can't imagine this was actually the work of aliens."

"Do you think it was the work of magic?" Jake asked gently. "Because this is a massive field. I don't know if it's even possible to fake crop circles, but if it is, this would likely take a really long time."

I glanced out at Gus's field, searching for any hint of magic as I'd done before but, again, came up with nothing.

"I still don't see any evidence that someone did this magically," I said. "But I could be wrong. I'll call Renée and see if she can check it."

As I texted Renée, I realized I hadn't asked Neve if there was a possibility Marty had died by magic. Sure, he was stabbed, but was the knife controlled magically, perhaps? I pulled out my phone and texted her.

> Marty's injuries were purely from the knife, right?

The little bubbles came almost instantly, indicating she was responding.

NEVE

> Yes. NM

NM meant no magic. We'd developed a bit of a shorthand in case our phones were ever gone through. Granted, anyone could figure out what NM meant if they thought about it hard enough.

> When you were at the crime scene, did you recognize anything special about the crop circles?

> No. It had to be aliens.

Her following text was the winky face emoji with the

tongue sticking out.

I laughed and then switched over to text Renée.

Would you come by Gus's house at some point and inspect it for magic?

No bubbles appeared. Renée usually took a while to get back to me. She was swamped as the interim Grand Witch of the States. Just like I would be when I finally moved into the position.

My stomach tightened at the thought, but I pushed it away. It was something I had to do. End of story.

"Everything okay?" Jake asked, watching me from the open garage door.

"Sorry," I said, coming out of my thoughts. "I was messaging Renée. What are you looking for in here?"

I walked into the garage after Jake, allowing my eyes to adjust to the darkness. I was happy Penelope hadn't followed me in here. There were probably about a dozen ways she could get hurt between all the sharp edges and the various liquids on the floor.

"Kitty litter," Jake said. "But from the looks of things, Gus has been lazy about cleaning up."

"That doesn't mean there wasn't kitty litter in here, just that he hadn't been using it."

"Right," Jake said. "But there would have had to have been a large amount used for the amount of blood Marty lost. We have to figure out where it would have been disposed."

Penelope wailed outside. Then I heard a scream. I bolted from the garage to see what was the matter.

13

Penelope continued squealing as she chased an enormous man toward us through the middle of the cornfield. It looked like they'd come from a small grove of trees on the far side of the property.

"Make it stop," the man yelled. As he came closer to us, I recognized him. It was Gorvich.

"Penelope, that's enough," I shouted. "Leave him alone."

But she didn't stop until Gorvich stood right in the middle of five police officers.

I scooped Penelope into my arms as Gorvich trembled in fear.

"What is wrong with that pig?" Gorvich yelled.

"She's usually not this aggressive," I said, though that was only partly true. She was that aggressive when she felt like someone was threatening her or someone she cared about. "What happened?"

"I was on a walk and I saw her and she ran up to me and started biting at my heels like one of those sheep herding dogs." He pulled one of his socks down to show where Penelope had bitten him.

"How about we retrace your steps?" I suggested. "Maybe you were getting close to something regarding the case, and Penelope didn't want you to mess up the crime scene."

Penelope oinked up at me as if I was on the right track.

"I don't think that'll be necessary," Gorvich said. "Look, I won't press charges for your animal attacking me. I'll just be on my way."

The officer closest to him wiggled his nose and sniffed hard enough we could hear him. "Why do you smell like bleach?"

Panic flashed in his eyes briefly before he took off running again.

Penelope wiggled in my arms, but I held tight. She might have been able to catch him if he'd gotten any farther, but the officer who had smelled him was prepared. He caught Gorvich's shirt like it was nothing, spun Gorvich around, and cuffed him against the police car next to them.

"It looked like they came from that grove of trees," I said.

"Let's go," Jake agreed.

"If I let you down, will you show us where you found him and not attack him again?" I asked Penelope.

Jake's gaze flicked to me, and I couldn't help but recognize the amusement on his face. He probably thought it was silly talking to Penelope, but I knew it wasn't.

Penelope looked up at me, her big blue eyes

connecting us, and let out a small oink. It was her word—a promise—that she wouldn't go after him again.

I put her on the ground, and she tore off toward the trees.

"Looks like she listened," Jake said, running after her.

I trotted behind him—there was no need to pass him up and make him feel like he was getting old.

Penelope disappeared between a few trees, and Jake followed closely behind.

I nearly gasped when I saw what she'd stopped next to —a half-bleached, half-bloody wheelbarrow.

"I guess we know how Marty was transported and where he was killed," I said, glancing down at the remaining bits of blood-soaked kitty litter.

"Do you see a knife anywhere?" Jake asked. "Maybe if we can find the knife, we can get some DNA evidence to catch our killer."

"I think we just caught him," I said. "Why else would Gorvich be out here cleaning a wheelbarrow?"

"Maybe he's covering for someone," Jake suggested.

"Then he'd know who that someone is because only the murderer knows where they tried to hide this. But it seems strange they wouldn't have gone through more trouble to dispose of the evidence. I know we hadn't yet, but in all likelihood, we would have found these things at some point."

"Maybe whoever did it thought they'd get away with bleaching it before we found it," Jake said. "Then it would have seemed like a random wheelbarrow sitting out in a grove of trees."

He had a point.

"I think Gorvich is as likely a suspect as Gus. Maybe even more likely, since he knew this was out here."

"Only one way to find out," Jake said. "Wanna join me?"

"Is that even a question?" I laughed. "Of course I do. Come on, Penelope."

Satisfied with herself, Penelope trotted ahead of us to Gus's driveway.

I kept my eye on the ground. How had we missed the rut made by the wheelbarrow? Especially one holding an entire body? I tried to remember what the weather had been like, but I'd been out of town. "Hey, when's the last time it rained?"

Jake thought about it for a minute. "Probably a little over a week ago. Why?"

"I was trying to figure out how we'd missed the wheelbarrow track. But if the ground wasn't hydrated, that could be part of the reason."

"And if they pushed the wheelbarrow over the stalks after they'd been pushed down into the crop circles, it wouldn't have been as noticeable either."

About halfway to the driveway, something bright green caught my eye. "Jake, come look at this."

He turned to me and squatted down by where I pointed. "Looks like a piece of rope—you know how threads come off occasionally?"

"Fran has this exact rope at her store," I said. "I bet she could tell us if someone purchased it recently."

"It's worth a shot," Jake said. "I'll hang out here so we don't lose the evidence. Would you mind asking an officer in the driveway to come over with the evidence kit?"

"Will do." Penelope and I finished the walk, then said to the closest officer, "Jake needs someone to bring the evidence kit out to where he is in the field. We may have found something important."

He nodded and hurried off to help Jake.

"Check this out," another officer said. "Look what the drone found."

I glanced at the tiny screen of his phone attached to a drone controller. The sun was so bright it made it hard to see over the glare. "I can't see anything."

"Here, hold the controls. Just don't push any buttons or move any joysticks."

I held the drone as gently as possible in my palms, keeping my fingers splayed so they wouldn't accidentally touch anything and cause the drone to come crashing into the earth.

"Those look like tire tracks," I said.

"Big tire tracks," the officer agreed.

"Do you know what kind of vehicle they're from? Or where they're located?" I glanced up into the sky, trying to see where the drone was, but before I caught a glimpse, the controller slipped from my hands and tumbled to the ground.

It was like the world went into slow motion.

The officer's voice made a long and drawn-out, "Noooooooo," as he tried to catch the controller before it hit the ground.

My scalp tingled with the hair change I didn't have the focus to stop.

I tried to catch it, but my hands collided with the officer's hands, preventing both of us from saving the device.

The crunch of the plastic on the gravel driveway made me cringe. I could only hope it wasn't damaged too badly.

Then I realized it wasn't only the controller we had to worry about.

I glanced at the officer who had picked up the controller and was trying desperately to make the buttons work while he searched the sky for the tiny flying object.

It wasn't until I saw the drone falling from the sky that I noticed where it was. We didn't hear the crash since it fell on the other side of the field.

"I am so sorry," I said.

"Come on. We need to go find it." The officer opened the passenger door for me—thankfully, the front seat and not the back—before running around to the driver's side and sliding in.

He tore out of the driveway as if someone's life depended on it. Heck, maybe it did. Maybe this guy would be fired for my mistake.

"I'll replace it," I said. "If it's broken. I can buy the department a new one."

"It's not about whether it's broken," he said. "If it fell into the creek, it could have damaged the footage we've taken from dozens of crime scenes."

"Why didn't you transfer the files to a computer before now?"

"I should have," he said. "But we never needed them and I'm behind on my reports and Jake is going to kill me."

"Slow down," I said. "Jake won't kill you. I crashed the drone. And I'm sure it didn't land in the creek."

We turned the corner, and I wished I hadn't uttered

those words.

There the drone was, smashed at the bottom of the nearly dry creek bed. Too bad the drone had fallen in the bit of water that still ran through the creek.

The officer shifted the car into park before it stopped, making it jolt, but he didn't seem to care. He tore off down the side of the creek, his uniform getting dusty from the slide.

He inspected the drone briefly before hugging it to his chest and yelling, "Nooooooo," again, as if his only child had been murdered.

I got out of the car, unsure how to help the poor man.

"Can I look at it?" I asked, sliding down the bank of the creek.

He swiveled his chest away from me like a child trying to keep their sibling from stealing their favorite toy.

"I can't hurt it any more than it is, can I?" I asked gently.

He studied me for a minute, then looked down at the drone. After what felt like a solid minute of silence, he held the drone out for me to see.

I had no idea how to fix a drone. I could hardly work my phone. But I did have healing magic. And if it worked on living things, why wouldn't it work on inanimate objects?

I closed my eyes and focused on the crumpled aircraft in my hands.

From the gasp that came from the officer, I figured something was happening. But it wasn't like healing something living because the drone didn't reciprocate with its pain or emotions.

Either way, when I opened my eyes, the drone was as good as new in my hands.

"Think you could do that to the controller, too?" the officer asked.

"I can give it a shot," I said.

He looked like he might hug me.

"Don't be too excited," I said. "I fixed the device, but the files might have been damaged permanently."

His expression drooped.

We scurried up the side of the creek, and I did the same thing with the controller as I had with the drone. It came out looking like new.

"It looks better than when we bought it," the officer said.

"You see if the footage is still there," I said. "I'll check on that tire track."

He nodded, though I was reasonably certain he didn't care what I did at that moment. His primary focus was the footage.

I walked to the edge of the field where the bent crops met the gravel road and found the tire tracks stuck in the mud. I sighed. These couldn't have been from the same night. If the wheelbarrow hadn't made noticeable divots in the dirt, there was no way these perfect tire tracks would have been made in the same dry dirt.

The officer had a big smile on his face when I returned. "The files are all there. You did it. Thank you."

I held up a hand to stop him from hugging me. "I don't think those tire tracks are from the night of Marty's murder."

The officer looked at me, stunned. "What do you mean

you don't think they were from the night Marty was murdered?"

"They came from mud," I said. "And Jake said it hadn't rained in at least a week. If there was only dry dirt, there couldn't have been mud that night to make those tracks."

"I see what you're saying, but you're not looking at the entire picture," he said. "Come on. I'll show you."

I followed him to the tire tracks.

"See, this corner of the property is the lowest," he said, pointing at the house uphill from where we stood. "You're from Colorado, right?"

"Yeah." I shifted from one foot to the other. "But why does that matter?"

"I think it's something to do with groundwater. Have you heard of groundwater?"

"I went to school," I said. "Of course, I've heard about groundwater."

"Right, but there's not a lot in Colorado, at least not as much as in Iowa. I think that's part of why they have the fires in Colorado and why we can burn our ditches with little thought here."

It sounded like he was making all of this up, but he had a point about the fires. When I first moved to Iowa, I was terrified about all the intentionally started fires. If you so much as dropped a lit cigarette out your window in Colorado, you could destroy entire forests and communities.

"But what does that have to do with the tire tracks?"

"The creek still has some water in it," he explained. "I'd venture to guess that if we dug into the soil here—

near the tire tracks—we'd find softer ground than we'd find up by the house."

"And with the weight of a truck that big, they'd have easily gone through the first layer of soil," I said, glancing down. Then I saw the final indicator that at least part of the tracks was made after the corn had been pushed down. "Look over here. The tire track goes through the field as if they made a U-turn instead of backing onto the gravel. And it goes directly over bent corn stalks."

"So this could be our killer, crop circle maker, or both."

"Or neither," I said. "It could have happened any time afterward, too. With all the press eager to get a story, I could see them coming down here to get a unique shot."

"In a massive truck?"

"Who knows?" I bent down to touch the corn stalks stuck in the tire tracks. "If only I could sense things from the corn."

"Your magic fixed the drone. Maybe it can do more than you think it can."

My scalp tingled with anticipation. Maybe I could.

I closed my eyes and focused. What kind of vehicle did this? Though possibly still alive, the corn apparently had no way of actually talking to me.

Just as I was about to give up, the officer beside me screamed.

My eyes shot open to see an unusual sight.

The corn had all stood back up.

"Ellie!" Jake's yell came from the center of the field.

Not only had I healed the crop, I'd destroyed the crime scene.

14

I touched the cornstalks again to make them return to how they were, but apparently, my magic only worked for healing.

"I'm sorry," I yelled. "I didn't mean to."

Jake didn't reply.

Shoot.

He was probably furious with me.

Penelope, who I'd left up at the house with Jake and the other officers, came squealing through the corn toward me.

"I'm right here," I said, trying to give her a direction to get to me. My guess was she wandered a bit too far away. Then when the corn popped up, she was stuck smack in the middle, unsure where to go. "It's okay, come this way."

She barreled out from between the cornstalks and straight into my arms. She wiggled her snout all over my face as if giving me kisses. Normally, this would make me laugh. But right now, I could only think about how mad Jake was. And how badly I'd messed up the case.

"Let's get up there," the officer I'd driven down to the edge of the field said.

I'd almost forgotten he was there. "Okay."

"Don't worry, we all mess up. Jake's pretty forgiving."

"Says the guy who thought Jake would kill him for breaking a drone," I said.

"That's fair."

We drove to the house, and Jake met us in the driveway.

"Why did you do that?" Jake asked. "You practically tampered with the entire crime scene in one fell swoop."

Penelope grumbled at him from my arms.

"It's okay, Penelope." I turned my focus to Jake. "I'm really sorry. I didn't mean to do it at all. I used my magic to fix—uh—" I glanced at the officer whose drone I'd broken. "—something else, and I think it was in overload. When I touched the corn, it healed the entire field."

"I'd say that's pretty impressive," the officer with the drone said. He was trying to help—probably since I hadn't thrown him under the bus about the drone—but Jake didn't seem pleased by him coming to my defense.

"I tried to make it go back the way it was," I said. "But I don't think my magic works that way. It can only fix things and people, not break them."

Jake closed his eyes and rubbed a hand over his forehead. "I know it was an accident, but who knows what evidence this might have disturbed? And I don't even know how I'll explain to the district attorney, judge, or jury that the crop magically came back to life."

Not everyone knew there was magic in the world. Cliff Haven residents—Cliffers—typically did, but I suppose that didn't mean that magic was included in any of their police procedures or law books.

"Maybe a magical lawyer can work alongside the district attorney as an expert to explain that my magic did nothing to wreck the crime scene other than fix the corn."

"Do you know that for sure?" Jake asked, his face stuck in a worried frown.

"No," I admitted. "I don't. But I could have Renée—if she'd ever text me back—come help determine that."

Jake considered this. "I'll figure it out. We were pretty close to being done with the scene anyway, and thankfully, I got photos of the wheelbarrow and that scene before this happened, too."

"We also saw huge tire tracks that went through the field after the corn had been flattened," the officer held out the drone controller to Jake to show him the footage. "See how the muddy tire tracks incorporate the cornstalks that have been bent like the others?"

"That's something," Jake said. "But it could be nothing, too. Teenagers love to hang out on gravel roads. And there have been lots of looky-loos lately who might have been trying to get a good look at the crop circles. That would make a pretty good vantage point."

I nodded. I knew all of that, but hearing him confirm it sent my spirits plummeting even further. If only I hadn't touched the stupid cornstalk. Ugh.

"Why don't you guys wrap up the scene," Jake said. "Ellie and I will head to the station to talk to Gorvich."

The other officers nodded and shot me glances of sympathy.

Penelope nuzzled into me.

"I'll take Penelope home, and then I'll meet you down there," I said.

Jake nodded and got in his car without another word.

I waited until I had Mona backed out and pointed away from the officers before I let the tears run down my cheeks. Just when I thought I had my magic under control, it did something like this.

Mona's steering wheel warmed beneath my grip as if trying to comfort me.

First, I couldn't control my magic—my color-changing, shape-shifting hair being a liability my entire life. Now, I still couldn't control it only in the opposite way. And even though it was doing something good—healing a crop—it still hurt someone I cared about and possibly destroyed evidence that would have helped us solve a murder case.

The tears kept coming as I drove Mona directly into the garage. I didn't want to have to come into contact with any of the squatters camping in my field. Maybe when they were done, I could use my magic to heal my beans so I'd have a successful crop this year, too.

"Why are you crying?" an ethereal voice came from behind me as I snuck into the backdoor carrying Penelope.

I turned to see Esme in all her shimmering glory behind me.

"I thought I could control my magic, but it turns out I can't."

"That's nonsense," Esme said. "I've seen you control your magic. What happened? Is this about your hair?"

I pulled a curly tendril from my head to see it. In all the stress, my hair had changed. I didn't even have the heart to put it back as it was supposed to be.

Instead, I grabbed a scarf from a basket I kept on the kitchen counter full of knick-knacks I needed daily, like chapstick and a phone charger, and tied it over my hair to hide it. There were too many out-of-towners for me to be parading around with my strange hair.

"Ellie?" Esme asked again. "What happened?"

"I ruined Jake's crime scene by fixing the corn," I said. "And now we might never figure out who killed Marty."

"You fixed an entire crop of corn without trying?" Esme asked.

"I'd fixed a drone and a drone controller right before that. I think I had focused my magic on fixing mode, so when I touched the corn, it fixed that too," I said. "I didn't realize I'd have to turn my magic off after using it."

"Normally, one doesn't have to," Esme said. "And what's a drone?"

"It's a small flying object people use to get photos and videos from overhead. I think people use them to race and stuff too, but I don't know."

"And you fixed this small, inanimate object?"

"Yes," I said. "It's the first time my magic worked to fix something not living."

"That's some pretty advanced magic," Esme said. "Something your mother never even mastered."

A knot tightened in my stomach. I made a mental note not to get too close to Gerald if I visited before he died. My magic might go into overdrive and fix him without me even trying. Though I liked the idea of healing people, I always wanted to make sure I asked for their consent first.

"Don't worry about it," Esme said. "Jake's been through harder cases than this. Remind him of the time he accidentally knocked over an entire five-gallon bucket of oil, completely taking out every piece of evidence the officers had marked but hadn't yet photographed. He still solved that case."

I smiled. "Thanks, that makes me feel better."

"No really, remind him, then tell me what his face looks like when you do."

I had a feeling when Esme and Jake worked together, the power dynamic was slightly different between the two of them than it was between him and me. She was likely the expert, as he was a new officer. Now, he was the chief of police, and I was the newbie.

"I don't think I'll bring it up. But it does make me feel better that I'm not the only one who messes things up sometimes."

"Not in the least. I have plenty of stories where that came from. Have you heard anything from Xander?"

I needed to get down to the police station to help Jake, but I also wanted to run my thoughts by Esme. "I've been thinking a lot about that," I said quickly. "I think I'll let Emily stay the way she is."

Esme didn't look at all stunned by this declaration. "I wondered if you'd decide that."

"I don't think it's fair to go against her wishes, forcing her memory on her," I said. "It seems a bit too selfish to upend her entire life just so I can have a mom. I've gone this many years without one. At least now I know who she is. She and I can be friends—I can visit her diner sometimes."

"That's very mature of you." Esme paused and gave me a thoughtful look. "But I know—knew—Emily pretty well. And though I agree, I think it should be her decision whether she wants her memories back. The Emily I knew would never miss a chance to know you as her daughter. She sacrificed everything to save you, which means she'd want to do everything to know you now that the threat has been neutralized."

"But how can I get her approval to give her back her memories without asking her and exploding her brain?" I asked.

Esme shrugged. "I'm sure you'll figure out a way."

"I'll have to figure it out later. I'm heading to the police station to get a guy to confess that he killed some-one, effectively nullifying my mistake."

"That's a lot of pressure to put on yourself and him," Esme said. "Who did they end up catching?"

"You've probably seen him around here—Gorvich—the leader of one of the cohorts."

"Oh yeah, he didn't murder the guy," she said as if that was common knowledge.

"What do you mean? How do you know?"

"He has an alibi," Esme said. "Everyone out there is pointing fingers at everyone else. The guy who died used to be part of their cohort but was kicked out. I don't know. But at least a dozen people have asked Gorvich where he was that night, and he was at a high-profile dinner with a dozen other lawyers in Chicago. He has receipts, witness statements, and social media proof he was there."

"Wait, Gorvich is a lawyer?" I asked.

"Apparently, a pretty good one, too," Esme said, nodding. "I bet he's bailed out before the day ends."

"Maybe I don't need to go down there after all," I said.

"Just because he wasn't there doesn't mean he won't know anything," Esme said. "Get your tiny little butt down to that station. He's the leader of a group that Marty was kicked out of. There has to be a story there somewhere."

She was right. I couldn't not go. Even though I wanted to avoid Jake at all costs.

15

I pulled up to the police station to find a group of people in the parking lot arguing. A group of people I knew.

Jasmine and Gus stood next to each other as Jasmine yelled at Gorvich and who I assumed was his attorney.

They didn't seem to realize I was the one in the microbus. I rolled my window down slightly to listen.

"You didn't fire me. I quit," Jasmine shouted.

"You were a terrible attorney," Gorvich replied, his voice not quite at a yell but definitely raised. "I'm surprised you got this guy out at all. And how did you even make bail?"

"I have plenty of money," Jasmine said. "And Gus is going to help me start my firm."

"About that," Gus said.

"Uh-oh," Gorvich said.

"You can leave," Jasmine said. "This is not a conversation you need to be privy to."

"Then don't have it in public," Gorvich said.

Jasmine groaned.

"I only told you those things so you'd help me get out." Gus shrugged as Jasmine's face wrinkled into the meanest scowl I'd ever seen.

"You lied to me?" Jasmine grumbled.

Gus shrugged. "You should have known better."

Jasmine's eyes widened. "You'll regret this, old man. You'll stand trial for this crime, and I won't be here to defend you."

"There's always a public defender. They'll probably do a better job if I believe what Gorvich said." Gus looked downright smug at the trick he'd pulled on his daughter.

Gorvich also looked smug. And his attorney.

Part of me wanted to get out of Mona and give Jasmine some backup or moral support. But I had a feeling it wouldn't be well received.

I didn't have time, anyway. Jasmine stormed off to her fancy car and squealed from the parking lot.

"You're gonna regret that," Gorvich said, his voice higher pitched to mock Jasmine.

"The only thing I regret is telling her before she took me home. I was itching for a ride in that car. And the farm's so far away."

"We'll give you a lift," Gorvich said, glancing at his attorney, who nodded.

Gus, Gorvich, and the attorney walked away as if they were best friends and nothing had happened with Jasmine.

Wow, Gus was a horrible father.

Once they were gone, I took a deep breath and went inside.

Jake greeted me in the lobby.

"Did you catch any of that?" I asked.

Jake nodded. "Security cameras."

"Right," I said. "I only caught the last half. What started the argument?"

"Jasmine used to work at Gorvich's firm," Jake said. "When they saw each other, it was an instant argument."

"I assume you got Gorvich's alibi?"

"Yep," Jake said. "He wouldn't have talked to us, anyway. He knows his rights probably better than we do."

"Nah," I said. "You guys know a lot."

"Sorry you had to come down here," Jake said. "It looks like we'll have to keep collecting evidence until trial."

"I'm surprised the judge let Gus out on bail," I said.

"Not enough evidence to support that he did it," Jake said. "Plus, he's wearing an ankle monitor. We'll know where he goes, anyway."

"Could he take it off?" I asked.

"We'd be alerted, and it likely wouldn't be hard to catch up with him."

"All right," I said. "If that's all."

"I'm sorry I got angry with you at the scene."

"You had every right to be mad," I said. "I didn't know it would happen, but I'll be much more careful in the future. I shouldn't have been touching potential evidence, anyway."

"Not all the corn needed to be evidence. Just because it

was stuck in a tire track didn't make it evidence, either. You weren't doing anything wrong."

"But I messed everything up," I said, trying to keep the emotion from coming out in my voice.

"We were done processing the scene," Jake said. "I just didn't want to open it up for Jasmine to take over."

"But it's Gus's house," I said. "And it's obvious she's not welcome there."

"Jasmine is his daughter, though," Jake said. "I'm sure she knows where all the keys are hidden to get inside."

"Gus sounds like a total jerk," I said. "He used her to get out of jail."

"I still can't wrap my head around why he wouldn't have used the appointed council," Jake said. "He's used them in all of his other cases."

"How successful were they?"

Jake smirked. "Not terribly."

"That's probably why. And Jasmine had the motivation to do a good job. Gorvich said she wasn't a good lawyer, but it sounds like she's good enough."

"She's very good. Gorvich doesn't want to admit it because that would mean he was wrong to fire her."

"Then I'm sure she'll start her firm eventually, even without Gus's help."

Jake shrugged. "We may never know. I'd guess she won't be returning to Cliff Haven."

"I think that's a pretty good guess." I checked my watch. "You know what? Fran's probably still open. I can talk to her about the rope if you want me to."

"That would be great," Jake said. "Report back about what you find. I have a lot of paperwork to catch up on."

I left the station and hopped into Mona. I felt slightly better besides the fact we hadn't gotten any information out of Gorvich. However, Gus as the murderer felt right. Now, we had to prove he did it.

"There's my favorite witch. Whatcha doing?" Fran said when I walked in. The kitty I'd snuggled before sat on the counter and perked up at the sight of me.

"I'm trying to sort out this case," I said, scratching the kitty behind the ears. "And I thought you might help me?"

"I'll do what I can," Fran said. "Not that I know much about these cases you find yourself in the middle of."

"I think you might have some expertise with this. You know that neon green rope you sell? Have you had anyone buy some recently who wouldn't usually buy it?"

"As a matter of fact, we did." Fran glanced around. "But I don't think the person who bought it is responsible for murdering Marty."

"It's a lead we're following. It could be nothing." I glanced down the aisle where the spool had been. "Did they buy a lot? I don't see it down there anymore."

"They bought several yards," Fran said.

"Did they buy anything else?"

Fran shifted her weight from one foot to the other.

The kitty stretched one leg out to my stomach then climbed its front paws up to my chest with its back paws still on the counter.

"I know this is hard," I said over the kitty's loud purrs. "You don't want to get anyone in trouble. And maybe they're not in trouble. Maybe this is all a mix up. But I have to check into it, you know?"

"That's only part of the reason I'm agitated." She

shook her head. "I should have realized the combination of things I was selling might have been a problem."

My heart rate sped and the kitty's kneading intensified on my shoulder. "What else did they buy?"

"A gallon of neon green paint, some screws, a tiny green lightbulb, and a burner phone."

16

My eyes went to the pegboard behind the counter where one of the burner phones were missing.

"Only criminals need burner phones," Fran repeated what Katie had said.

"Not necessarily," I said, trying to ease her anxiety. "There could be a good reason for it."

"It was a local teenager," Fran said. "Clark Russell. His dad's a farmer, and his mom does in-home childcare. He put it on his dad's account so I assumed it was for his dad, but maybe it wasn't."

My mind went to the kids at the café. The ones with the massive trucks with massive tires. "Does he drive one of those big trucks?"

She nodded. "He and his friends do."

That meant the kids from the café were likely the ones who had created the crop circles, called it in to the police, and could have either committed the murder or seen who did.

"Thank you for your help," I said, kissing the kitty on the head and returning its front paws to the counter.

"Here's their address." Fran scribbled it on a piece of receipt paper she'd gotten from the register receipt roll. "Clark should be home by now. School ends at three."

"It's already past three?" I asked. The day had gotten away from me. "I better get going. I'm burning daylight."

Fran smiled. "Thanks for stopping in. It's always good to see your smiling face."

"Tell Amy I say hi." I turned to the kitty. "Bye, kitty."

Once I was back in Mona, I told her the address. "Let's not go fast. Just get me there as if I were driving."

Mona took control and slowly eased us down the road to a farm a few miles away.

Two massive trucks with oversized tires sat in the driveway beside a minivan. The trucks weren't clean like they'd been when parked outside of Katie's Café. They had mud and cornstalks caked between the aggressive tire grooves and to the sidewalls. If these boys were trying to hide what they'd done, they weren't doing a very good job.

I knocked on the door and heard an uproar of little voices coming from inside.

A woman with dark brown hair pulled into a severe bun on her head answered. "Can I help you?" Her voice was sweet. Children peeked around her and clung to her legs.

"I'm Ellie Vanderwick," I said. "I'm helping the police with a case right now."

Her eyes widened. "The one from Gus's place?"

I didn't want to say anything traumatizing in front of the kids, so I just nodded.

"Is there something I can do for you? I didn't know Marty."

"I'm here to speak to your son—Clark—I think he might have seen something that night." I didn't want to go down the route of accusation yet. Especially since she could slam the door in my face and refuse to let me speak to him.

"I'm sure he'd be happy to help," she said. "I'll get him. If you'd like to meet him at the picnic table on the backside of the house, that would be great."

"Thank you."

She closed the door gently, careful not to catch any little fingers, and I walked to the back of the house.

A couple of dogs barked in the distance. I closed my eyes and let my skin soak up the breeze and sun.

"Uh, are you the lady who wanted to talk to me?" A tall teenage boy wearing a baseball cap and jeans asked. He and another—shorter—boy dressed almost the same way walked toward me. They probably thought I was a weirdo standing there with my eyes closed and a smile on my face.

"Are you Clark?" I asked.

"I am," the boy said. "This is Billy."

"I'm Ellie. I've seen you in the diner a few times."

"Wasn't it you who told us to be nice to Gus the other night?" Clark asked.

"That's me," I said. "But I have a feeling you weren't all that nice to Gus after that, were you?"

They exchanged glances but said nothing.

"Look," I said. "I know you created the crop circles. My guess is you wore green suits and made sure all your equipment was green so you could edit it from the drone footage you'd taken. Oh, and the green light on the drone was a nice touch."

"I don't know what you're talking about," Clark said.

"Really?" I raised my eyebrows in the best questioning glance I could create. "I guess I can call Jake over here, and he can search your trucks and houses. The mud and cornstalks still caked to the sides of your tires is a dead giveaway that you drove through Gus's field after the circles were created."

I pulled my phone out of my leather satchel and started to call Jake.

"Okay, stop," Billy said. "We can't get in any more trouble. I'll tell you what you want to know."

17

I returned my phone to my satchel and waited for them to talk.

Billy spoke after a few seconds. "We probably shouldn't have done it, but Gus is horrible. And it's hilarious to get him worked up. You saw him at the café. It was too easy. All we had to do was make it look like aliens had come, and he'd probably start running up and down the streets in his underwear and a tinfoil hat."

"Either way, it was stupid," Clark said. "But, yeah, we did it. We made the circles and the video and posted them on of the closest alien fanatic groups. We didn't think anyone would die."

"So you're saying you didn't kill Marty?"

They both gaped at me.

"You think we killed him?" Clark asked, his voice squeaking halfway through the question.

"You were out there when he was murdered. You called the police to report it on your burner phone. Either you did it, and you're covering for one another, or you saw who did."

"No," Clark said. "No way. We didn't kill him. We saw him and Gus fighting on Gus's steps and wanted to freak them out a bit. Gus ran inside, but the other guy—Marty—walked toward us. He asked us to take him with us. He really thought we were aliens."

"We were pretty realistic-looking," the other boy said.

"But then something else caught his attention, and he ran off toward a bunch of trees. We hurried and finished the circles before getting out of there."

"And the phone call?" I asked.

"We were calling to report the crop circles," Billy said. "We weren't reporting a murder."

"Do you know what caught Marty's attention?" I asked. It had to be something insanely interesting to draw him away from the aliens.

"No idea," Clark said.

The other boy shook his head, answering my question.

"What about your friends who were with you?" I asked. "There was a drone. Maybe they caught something on the footage?"

"If we show you, will it keep us out of trouble?" Clark asked, glancing at his house.

I didn't have the authority to make any deals. "I'll see what I can do."

They looked at each other, unsure.

"Until you can tell me for sure, I'm not bringing anyone else into this. I'm not a rat. And that means not giving you the footage either because it'll show them and their vehicles," Clark said.

"That's fair," I said. "Let me make a call real quick."

I walked away so they wouldn't hear me beg Jake.

"Hello?" Jake said when he answered the phone. "Is everything okay?"

"All good," I said. "I'm over at Clark Russell's house talking to him and a friend of his named Billy."

"What took you there?"

"I can give you the entire story later," I said. "But basically, they are the ones who created the crop circles. They say they didn't kill anyone and didn't see anyone kill anyone, but they have drone footage, and more friends were there."

"Did you ask them for the footage and to call the friends over?"

I left a pause.

"Of course you did. Sorry. Go on."

"They want to make a deal," I said. "They don't want to be held accountable for the destruction of the field."

"What destruction? The field looks healthier than it has in a decade," Jake teased.

I'd forgotten about healing the crop. They, obviously, hadn't heard that everything was back to normal.

"Does that mean they have a deal?" I asked.

"That means you can make it seem like they have a deal," Jake said. "But really, there's no reason I'd charge them now. If I did anything, I'd scare them so they don't do it again."

"Understood," I said. "Thank you."

"Good work," Jake said. "Do you need me over there for backup?"

"I think I have it under control," I said. "But if there's

anything on the drone footage, I'll bring it in for evidence."

"Your mom would be so proud of you. I hope you know that," Jake said.

I swallowed. The Emily ordeal was the last thing I needed to think about right now. I thanked him quickly, then hung up.

Before I returned to the boys, I steadied myself and cleared my throat.

"What did he say?" Billy asked.

Clark nudged him in the ribs as if telling him to act natural. They'd probably discussed how they would play it cool until they heard what I had to say.

"He said as long as you tell me everything you know—all of you—and show me the completely uncut drone footage, I can let you off with a warning."

"But what about Gus's crop?" Billy asked. "My dad said he'd be furious if someone did that to our crop."

"Gus can afford it," Clark said. "He doesn't farm it himself, and the money he makes from renting it out probably looks like pennies compared to what he made in the lottery a few years ago."

"Gus won the lottery?" I asked.

"Before he went to jail this last time," Clark said.

And here he was, saying he couldn't afford an attorney. Maybe that was part of the reason Jasmine was angry with him and refused to be his lawyer again.

"Either way," I said. "You have a deal. No charges will be filed. You're in the clear. But if this happens again, you'll be in even more trouble than you would be right now."

They looked at each other, then nodded. "Deal," they said in unison.

It only took about fifteen minutes for them to get the other three members of their group together. As we waited, parents arrived to pick up the daycare kids until all the kids were gone.

"You can come inside now if you'd like," Clark's mom said, peeking out the back door. "I can make some sandwiches."

The boys cheered.

"That'll make it easier to show you the drone footage," Clark said. "We have a big TV."

He wasn't joking. The TV was probably as long as Mona. It took up an entire wall.

While he plugged it in, I started talking.

"All right," I said, bringing my hands together, effectively quieting the five teenage boys. "I need your help to solve this case. Anything you might have seen that night could be the break in the case we need."

I knew that could go one way or the other: They'd either think it was cool or stupid to help solve a crime. Thankfully, they seemed eager to help.

"I don't think I saw anything," a boy with a buzz cut wearing a hoodie said. "The green suits were hard enough to move in, but having them over our faces was brutal."

"That's because you had yours on backward," another boy in a t-shirt with the arms ripped off said, laughing.

Buzz Cut punched T-shirt, and T-shirt acted like it didn't hurt even though I could see the bruise forming already.

"The rest of us had green face paint," Clark said. "We

had to be in all green—like a green screen. It made it easy to edit out our bodies and the equipment to make a video that looked like the circles were forming on their own."

"Like aliens were doing it with their mind control," T-shirt said.

"The video was compelling," I said. "And the costumes made Gus and Marty think you were aliens."

"We didn't think that part through, but it was icing on the cake," the fifth boy—the leader of the pack with his letterman jacket and extra swagger—said.

They all high-fived and laughed.

I could only imagine how funny that might have been seeing Gus's face when he thought aliens were emerging from his cornfield.

"Okay, we're good to go," Clark said, standing behind the sofa facing the TV and holding a remote.

I turned around and backed up a bit to watch.

The screen quality was top-notch. The green spotlight helped illuminate everything that happened. I focused on the patch of trees where we'd found the wheelbarrow.

At first, the boys sat still, watching me watch the video. But eventually, when I didn't make any comments, they lightened up.

"That's when I totally almost fell into the creek," T-shirt said.

"Here comes the part with Gus," Letterman said.

They all laughed and begged Clark to back it up and show it again.

He glanced at me, and I nodded in approval. I wanted to see what happened with Marty again.

The first time it had gone by pretty quickly. He and

Gus were arguing on the porch, then Gus went inside while Marty started into the field. Within seconds, though, he was distracted and ran off toward the trees.

They watched and laughed again, but the scene looked the same as before. I couldn't see anything in the trees.

"Do you think you could zoom into the trees?" I asked.

"I'll try," Clark said.

He did, but the footage became too grainy.

"Did you see that?" T-shirt whispered to Letterman.

"The flash of light?" Letterman said as if it was nothing.

"Boobs," T-shirt whispered even more quietly.

Too bad for him, I had excellent hearing. Plus, at the mere mention of boobs, all the boys were instantly more engaged.

"Uh, I'll rewind it one more time." Clark shrugged. "If there are boobs, that would explain the distraction."

He was right, but it felt weird to be looking for boobs with a bunch of teenage boys.

I shook my head. It was probably nothing. They were seeing what they wanted to see, not the other way around.

But when Clark stopped the video, there were definitely boobs in the trees. Big boobs.

I stepped closer, obstructing the view. The boys grumbled in annoyance, but I didn't care. I had to see if there was a face that went along with the chest.

No such luck. If I thought it was possible to only have a set of boobs without a body, I'd guess that's what was happening here. And maybe that was precisely what was happening. It would be a relatively surefire way to lure a man into a bunch of trees.

"What are you watching?" Clark's mom asked from behind me, her voice high-pitched.

I jumped about a foot off the ground, and all the boys were startled, too, quickly grabbing their phones and acting as if they hadn't been ogling the obvious bare chest on the screen. "It's the drone footage from a couple of nights ago," I explained. "This may explain why or how Marty was killed."

"Well, I'd appreciate it if you wouldn't show things like that to teenage boys. I think it's time you leave, Miss Vanderwick."

She had every right to kick me out. I nodded and started toward the door.

"Ellie didn't do it, Mom," Clark said. "I took the footage."

"And I spotted the boobs," T-shirt said.

Letterman stood from the couch. "We need her to stay so she can hear what we saw that night, and we can go through the rest of the footage. We welcome it if you want to stay and supervise, but please let us finish."

Mrs. Russell seemed torn, but Letterman and the other boys smiled at her, practically batting their eyelashes.

I couldn't believe they were standing up for me.

"Okay, fine," Mrs. Russell said. "But I'm staying to supervise. And get that off my screen. You know there were boobs in the trees—fake ones if you ask me."

I glanced at the TV before Clark fast-forwarded and took the zoom to normal range. How could she tell they were fake boobs?

18

Though they'd stood up for me, the teenage boys hadn't seen anything else that night. They hurried up and finished the job after they saw Gus.

"We thought he ran inside to call the police," Letterman said.

"Maybe Marty would still be alive if he had," Billy said.

We sat in silence, thinking about it.

"The rest of the footage is just of me landing the drone," Clark said.

"Could you send me a copy of the footage?" I asked.

"Yeah," Clark said. "Sorry it wasn't more helpful."

"I appreciate your cooperation," I said, looking at each of the boys individually, then at Mrs. Russell.

"If you ever need help with another case, let us know," T-shirt said, and the other boys nodded eagerly.

"I'll walk you out," Mrs. Russell said.

When we were almost at the door, I turned. "I'm sorry

the boys saw that. I had no idea that was what was actually in the trees."

"I overreacted," she said, glancing down at her feet. "I tend to be the overbearing mom."

"They all seem to adore you," I said. "I do have one question, though. What made you think the boobs on the screen were fake?"

"I had a double mastectomy a few years ago and then reconstruction surgery," she said. "The scars are easy to identify."

"So you think that was an actual, living woman? Not some sort of doll or something?"

"Yep," she said. "That was as real as they get. Well, as real and fake, I guess."

We laughed.

"Thank you again for understanding." I started out the door, but Clark called to me before I'd made it through.

"You might want to see this," he said.

The video was paused again on the screen, but from the kitchen, it was impossible to see what was there.

"It better not be more boobs." Mrs. Russell laughed.

The boys laughed too.

On the screen was the image of a car. A fancy, electric blue car. One I'd seen only once in Cliff Haven.

"Where was the car parked?" I asked.

"Just up the road from where we parked," Clark said. "Near the trees."

"Do you think it belongs to the woman who lured Marty away from the aliens?" Billy asked.

I sighed. "I'd absolutely say it did."

Once I was back in Mona, I called Jake.

"I think I know who did it," I said.

"So do we," Jake said. "We caught him red-handed."

"Him?"

"Gus," Jake said. "He killed Gorvich. We got an anonymous call about an argument at Gus's house. When we showed up, Gus was covered in blood trying to clean the knife in the sink."

"Are you certain it was him?" I asked. "Because I think it could have been Jasmine. Maybe she made the anonymous call."

"Jasmine's long gone," Jake said. "Already in the city. She posted on social media fifteen minutes ago with the Bean in the background."

"That could have been taken any time," I said. I didn't ask why Jake was stalking his ex's social media feed.

"We'll make the calls," Jake said. "But for now, Gus is our prime suspect. If Jasmine's responsible for anything, it's for helping him get out to kill again."

It didn't sit well in my stomach. Jasmine had lured Marty into the trees. The car was her car. There weren't any other cars like that or large-chested women who drove that specific car in Cliff Haven.

"Maybe they are working together," I said. "It would make sense."

"She had alibis, Ellie," Jake said, irritation creeping into his voice. "Gus did it."

"Do you need anything from me?" I asked, my tone clipped.

"No," Jake said. "I can take it from here."

We said our goodbyes and hung up.

If Jasmine was responsible for Gorvich's murder, she couldn't be far away.

I drove toward Gus's house, passing Jake on the way.

My phone rang. I didn't want to answer it. I could explain that I didn't want to be unsafe by using my phone while I drove. It was a copout, but I didn't have the energy to listen to his disapproving voice again.

Now that I was set on not trying to get Emily's memories back, I couldn't wait for Jake to marry Georgia. Then maybe his stress would melt away, and he'd return to his cheerful, happy-go-lucky self.

I told myself that if Xander and I ever got married, I'd keep my emotions under control. Then my mind came to a screeching halt.

If I didn't restore Emily's memories, I would be the next Grand Witch of the States. With Xander on the Magical Governing Council, we couldn't get married, let alone have a relationship. I took a deep breath and pushed the thought away. I'd leave it for another time. Right now, I needed to find Jasmine before she got away with killing —or helping kill—two men.

Gus's house was once again a full-on crime scene. I didn't even try to get inside. Jake had likely told everyone to keep me out anyway since I was off the case. It was fine by me. I didn't need to see another bloody crime scene.

I turned the corner to go down the road where Jasmine had been parked the first time. I'd unlikely catch her there again, but it was a good place to start.

As expected, the electric blue car was nowhere to be

found. I sighed. If I were her, I'd be on the fast track to Chicago to make some real alibis.

Would Gus flip on her? Tell the police that she was in on it? Or had she completely set him up? She told him he'd regret what he'd done. Maybe that was by framing him for murder. And Gorvich had fired her, which gave her motive.

What her motive would have been to kill Marty wasn't clear yet, but I was certain I could clear it up.

Now, I just needed to find her.

"Mona, it looks like we're heading to Chicago," I said as my phone chimed on the seat next to me. It was probably Jake, but I couldn't avoid him forever.

I picked it up to find three missed calls. One from Jake and two from Xander.

Jake had left a message. Xander hadn't.

I knew what Jake would say.

I tapped Xander's name to call him back.

"Thank goodness you called," Xander said. His voice was tired but urgent.

"What's wrong?" I asked.

"He doesn't have much time left. Mom and I want you to try again to convince him to accept the healing."

The case would have to wait. I needed to be there for Xander.

"I'll be there as soon as is magically possible," I said.

When we hung up, I decided to take Mona rather than teleport. It would be good to have her there if I needed a place to stay.

"Change of plans, Mona. Please take me to the hospital

where Gerald is," I said, tickling the dash. "As fast as you can."

She didn't hesitate.

We might have arrived more quickly than if I had teleported.

"Wow, that was intense," I said, steadying myself. "Thank you. I'll be back."

I hopped out and glanced out over the city. The sun was higher in the sky, perched atop the gorgeous Rocky Mountains. If I didn't need to hurry to help Gerald, I would have taken a photo.

Xander met me in the lobby and hugged me so tightly I could barely breathe. "Thank you for coming."

"Any time," I said. "Let's get up there and save your dad."

We walked hand-in-hand to the elevator, up to Gerald's floor, and down the hallway.

It surprised me to see Emily and Eloise standing on one side of the hallway with Xander's mom on the other. I didn't have time to make sense of it. A man was dying. A man who was important to so many people, even if he was a bit of a problem.

Emily smiled and gave me a quick hug. "Thank you for coming."

Elodie said nothing. She hadn't ever seemed to like me much.

Mrs. Wix nodded when I turned toward her. "Let's try this again."

I took a deep breath and followed her into the hospital room.

Gerald looked like a completely different person. A person who was about to die.

I hesitated for a second.

"What's wrong?" Xander asked.

"I don't want to heal him accidentally," I said. "I fixed the crop circle field with one touch and hadn't even been trying."

"Would it be so bad if you healed him without consent?" Mrs. Wix asked.

"If it's against his wishes, then yes," I said. "It's not my place to decide anything for anyone else."

"Just don't touch him," Xander said. "I'm sure it'll be okay."

I reached out a hand, and he took it. "Maybe my magic will stay calm if I'm connected to you."

Xander smiled and walked me to the bed. "Dad?" Xander said. "Ellie's here to see you."

"No," Gerald said, his words feeble. "No healing."

My magic coursed through me, eager to help. I shoved my free hand into my jacket pocket.

"I promise I won't heal you without your approval," I whispered.

"I am ready to die," Gerald said. "It's for the best."

"How is you dying for the best?" Mrs. Wix practically shouted.

"Mom," Xander said in a deep voice.

"Don't." She held a hand up to Xander. "He just found out he has a daughter. He has you. And many other things to live for. It's ridiculous he won't accept her healing."

"People are born, and people die," Gerald muttered.

"It's the way life goes. Just because we have magic doesn't make us immortal."

"I'm not asking for immortality. I'm asking for a few more years. Is that too much to ask?"

"Yes," Gerald said.

I leaned down, careful not to touch his skin. "I don't want my mother's memories to come back. I promise if I heal you, that won't even be a factor anymore."

He turned his head slowly. His gaze met mine. "Thank you for coming, but your services are not needed." He closed his eyes, but his chest continued to rise and fall. This wasn't up for negotiation. Gerald was going to die.

19

I walked from the room, defeated.

"It's not your fault," Xander said. "I shouldn't have called you away from the case."

"You absolutely should have," I said, turning to look at him. "You are more important to me than any case. And I want you to know that when I tell you what I have to tell you."

"I heard what you said to Gerald," he said. "I know what you're going to say. But right now, let's keep things as they are. You're not the Grand Witch yet, and I need you."

He bent down and kissed my lips gently, a buzz of electricity making my lips feel like I'd gotten injections to make my lips bigger like the girls on social media.

"Get a room," Eloise said.

"Eloise," Emily said, her voice kind but correcting.

Eloise glared at me, then stormed off, mumbling something about the vending machine.

"Xander, could you come in here for a moment?" Mrs. Wix asked from Gerald's doorway.

"I'll be here when you come out," I said, squeezing his hands.

He followed his mom, leaving Emily and me in the hallway together.

"It was lovely of you to come here for Xander," she said. "Isn't Iowa pretty far away?"

"Not as far as you'd think," I said. Emily didn't know any of us had magic. When she'd given up her memory, she'd also given up her magic and knowledge of the magical world.

"I wish there were something we could do for him," Emily said, absentmindedly pulling her bright white hair into a long ponytail.

I urged my hair to stay the same blonde as I'd fixed it to be before I'd walked inside. If it changed in front of her to be the exact color of hers, she'd freak out.

"Me too," I said. "But he seems pretty content with what's about to happen."

"I can't even imagine," Emily said, shuddering. "His poor family. And now Eloise. She's going through so many emotions about all of this. I should have told her years ago, but Gerald was a wild card. It was impossible to nail him down. I thought it would be better for her to have no father than it would to have a father who never showed up."

Fran's words popped into my head—ask the right questions.

"If she had the choice to know or not know, what would she have chosen?" I asked.

"She'd definitely have wanted to know," Emily said. "She and I are so different that way. I only wish I would have recognized that before right now."

"If you were in her shoes, you wouldn't want to know?"

She shook her head, her ponytail swishing behind her. "No way. I'd rather live in blissful ignorance than have my entire world turned upside down."

My breath caught in my throat. That settled it, then. I wouldn't try to get her memories back.

"And now he'll die, and she'll never get to know him. I'll have to live with that forever. I should have introduced them sooner."

"At least now she has a brother," I said. "I'm sure she was thrilled to know Xander was her brother."

"To be honest," Emily whispered, glancing down the hallway to make sure Eloise wasn't coming back, "I think she had a bit of a crush on him. Which made it slightly crushing when she found out they're related."

"Don't beat yourself up," I said. "You're an amazing mom."

"You're sweet," Emily said. "But you barely know me. I could be horrible behind the scenes."

"Nah," I said, trying not to internalize her comment. "I can tell. You have a good heart. You'd do anything to keep your daughter safe."

"You're right," Emily said, her gaze locking on mine. "I'd do anything for my daughter."

Chills ran down my arms, the hairs standing at attention.

"Everything okay?" Xander's voice broke the tension of the moment.

"Everything's fine," Emily said as if she hadn't noticed the tension. Maybe she hadn't. I mean, it wasn't like she knew I was her daughter.

Xander's hand slipped into mine and squeezed. "Where's Eloise?"

"She went to go get some snacks," Emily said. "I'm sure she'll be back soon."

"I don't think he has much longer," Xander said.

My heart ached as his sadness coursed through his hand into mine. Even though they weren't the closest, Gerald was still Xander's father.

Eloise came walking down the hallway holding a bottle of iced tea and a bottle of water. "I didn't know which one you'd want. I'll take whichever you don't," she said to Emily.

Emily smiled down at her daughter. "Thanks." She took the tea.

"Do you want to go in and see Gerald?" Xander asked Eloise. "I think we may be coming close to the end."

Eloise squared her shoulders and nodded. "Sure."

Xander started toward the door, pulling me along with him. I didn't budge from my spot. "I'll let the two of you go for now. I have to get home and check on Penelope."

Xander nodded in understanding before leaning down and kissing me on the forehead. "I'll let you know how it goes."

"I can be back in an instant," I said. "Just call."

"We can take care of him," Eloise said, grabbing the

hand I'd just dropped and pulling him toward their father's room.

"Bye," Xander said.

"I'm sorry about her," Emily said.

I turned to look at her. "You don't need to apologize. She has every right to feel whatever feelings she needs to feel right now."

"I hope we'll see you around," Emily said. "I know Xander really cares about you."

"I really care about him, too. And I will be in touch. Maybe I can win Eloise over, eventually."

"I'm sure you can."

I wanted to hug her. To squeeze her so tightly that she'd somehow remember me without me exploding her brain, but I held off.

"Tell Penelope we say hello," she said as I walked toward the elevator.

"I'll do that."

Once securely inside Mona, I let the tears flow freely. Gerald would die. My mother would never know me as her daughter. My sister might always hate me.

Mona's steering wheel warmed, sending comforting vibes through my veins. It would be okay. Emily had said it herself. She wouldn't want to know. She'd like to live in ignorant bliss. So ignorant bliss would be my gift to her.

"We need to go home and pick up Penelope," I said. "Then we're going to Chicago to find Jasmine. Or find out whatever we can about Jasmine."

Mona went into a hyper-speed mode, and we were on the gravel road to my house within minutes—she hadn't gone as fast this time, which was fine by me.

When we pulled into the driveway, a circle of people with candles stood in my field.

I hadn't even considered how these people would take the news that their leader had been killed. How selfish of me.

I parked Mona in the garage and let Penelope out before heading into the field to join their candlelight vigil. Without a word, a member brought me a candle and stood beside me as we listened to people tell stories about Gorvich. Penelope even wandered over after a little while and sat beside me, leaning against my legs.

The stories were about different times they'd gone to chase alien sightings—nothing of help regarding the case, but still interesting. When the vigil died down, the same person took my candle with a small smile and returned to the group. I took that as my prompt to head back to the house.

Since it had gotten late—I'd lost an hour going from Colorado to Iowa—I decided not to head to Chicago until early the following day. That didn't mean it would be easy to sleep.

After tossing and turning for what felt like forever, I headed to the attic to see if any of Esme's journal entries had revealed themselves. I tiptoed up the stairs as quietly as I could. I didn't want to wake Penelope. I couldn't even remember how long it had been since I'd come up here. Things had been all over the place lately with everything. I hadn't had much time to sit and read in my grandmother's journal.

The pages easily opened to a blank page. I tried to flip back, but every time they turned to the blank page.

The journal knew I needed to write.

So I did.

I wrote until my vision went blurry and my hand ached.

I wrote about Emily and Eloise, Xander and Gerald, and the case. I let the ink soak into the page and ensured my handwriting stayed as neat as possible.

And when my head felt like it had been squeezed out like a sponge, I stopped, placing the notebook and pen on the table next to the cozy chair where I sat.

The blanket around me was soft and snuggly. I didn't want to get up.

The next thing I knew, the sun was rising, and someone was whispering my name.

"Ellie. Ellie, wake up."

I opened my eyes to see Esme shimmering above me.

I sat up and moved my head from side to side, trying to work out the kinks from sleeping awkwardly. "What's up?"

"Your friends are downstairs with breakfast," she said. "I figured you might need some after the day you had yesterday."

I yawned. "Thank you."

"How are things with Gerald?" She followed me down the stairs into my bedroom.

"He won't make it much longer. If he's still with us

now." I glanced around my bedroom. "Where's Penelope?"

"She was making a ruckus at the top of the stairs, and Katie took her down. It's fun watching the gang together again. I miss those ladies."

"Do you want me to tell them anything?" I asked. "I could relay messages."

"Nah," she said. "I'm okay for now."

After taking a shower, I headed downstairs.

"Wow, what are you all dressed up for?" Nancy asked when I walked into the kitchen. People milled about the house, eating their breakfasts.

"I have to go to Chicago today to find someone," I said, glancing down at the pantsuit I'd put on. "Is it too much?"

"Not at all," Katie said. "It's the perfect outfit for the city. Who are you going to find?"

I glanced around to make sure no one besides my friends was listening. "Jasmine."

"Why?" Katie asked with a sour expression.

"I think she was either responsible or partially responsible for the two murders."

"But Jake arrested Gus," Nancy said.

"Did the boys tell you something?" Fran asked.

"They didn't tell me anything, but I saw something on their drone footage." I left out what exactly I'd seen. I didn't need to get into those details.

"Has Jake seen it?" Amy asked.

"I don't know. I sent it to him when I got it yesterday, but he seemed adamant about me leaving the case alone now."

"Ouch," Katie said. "I'm sorry, kiddo."

"It's all right," I said. "I think he's stressed about the wedding."

"I would be too with that woman as my future bride," Fran said.

"Bridezilla, you mean," Nancy said.

"I thought you guys liked Georgia," I said.

"That woman isn't Georgia. She's a mutation or something." Nancy laughed.

"Maybe it's a good thing," Katie said. "It'll make it clearer that Jake needs to be with Emily when she gets her memories back."

"About that," I said. "She won't get her memories back."

"But I thought you said—"

I held up a hand to stop Amy's sentence. "I've changed my mind." I explained to them why I'd changed my mind, including what Emily had told me at the hospital the night before.

"That's it? You're giving up?" Fran asked when I was finished.

"I'm not giving up," I said. "I'm letting things be the way they are. The way they're supposed to be."

"And you're okay becoming the Grand Witch?" Katie asked.

I nodded. "I am. It's in my blood."

20

I hopped into Mona, leaving Penelope with Katie and the others.

"All right, lady, let's go to Chicago." I tickled the dash, and Mona took off.

I had a plan—find Jasmine.

Plan B, if I couldn't find her, would be to find out everything I could about her. Jake may not think she had anything to do with this, but I had a feeling.

Mona drove into Chicago like she owned the place, swerving between cars and changing lanes like it was nothing.

"We'll go to the apartment building where she lived first," I said. "If I were her, that would be where I went."

Penelope drove right up to the front door of the high-rise apartment building, stopping in a no-parking zone.

"We need to park in a parking garage. I can't let you drive around without someone in the driver's seat."

Her engine sputtered in disappointment, but she took me to the parking garage across the street anyway.

"I'll be back," I said, grabbing my phone and slipping it into the fancy handbag I'd switched my satchel out for.

The apartment building door was locked with a list of tenant names and corresponding buttons to reach them on the intercom, presumably so they could buzz you in. I went down the list of names looking for Jasmine's, but none were even remotely similar.

Instead, I picked one at random.

"Hello?" a man's voice crackled through the speaker after a few seconds.

"Hi, I'm looking for Jasmine Norton," I said. "Do you know which apartment she's in?"

"Never heard of her," he said.

"Do you know someone who might?"

I realized he'd stopped listening.

I pushed another button. This time, no one answered.

The third button connected me with someone who spoke a language I didn't. But the fourth produced a woman who seemed willing to help.

"I don't think I've heard that name before," she said. "But I only moved in a couple of months ago."

Was it possible that Jasmine had moved and not left a forwarding address?

"Thank you," I said, ready to walk away and try Gorvich's firm. Surely someone there would know something about her, even if she hadn't worked there for a while.

But the woman's voice came back through the speaker, stopping me. "Come on in. We can talk to the maintenance guy. He knows everyone."

The speaker buzzed, and the door clicked. I pulled it open easily and walked inside.

A middle-aged woman with short, cropped hair came down the stairs with a big smile. "I'm Yoli."

I shook her hand. "Ellie. Thanks for your help."

"Sure thing," she said. "Do you mind if I ask why you're looking for Jasmine?"

"She was a friend of my mom's. They went to high school together. My mom died when I was a baby. I thought I'd try to catch up with some of her old friends to get to know her better." I wasn't about to tell a random woman—no matter how nice she seemed—why I was really there. Maybe she and Jasmine were close friends. She could easily be covering for her.

"That's nice," Yoli said, leading me down the stairs to the basement. "Where did your mom grow up?"

"Cliff Haven, Iowa," I said. "It's a super small town. Most people haven't heard about it."

"I grew up in a small town, too," she said. "They're not for the faint of heart."

"That's for sure," I said, even though I hadn't grown up in a small town.

We stopped at a door with a placard that read —Janitorial.

Yoli knocked. "You in there?"

The door swung open to reveal a short man with graying brown hair and a smile. "What's up?"

"This lady's looking for someone named Jasmine —uh?"

"Jasmine Norton," I said. "I heard she lived here at one point."

"The attorney?" His smile faltered. "Why are you looking for her? You in trouble? I can recommend someone better. That girl never won a single case."

"Oh," I said. "No. I was trying to catch up with her because she was friends with my mom. It's a long story. But does she still live here?"

"Nope. Yoli moved into her apartment."

Yoli's face lit up as if this was a happy surprise. "She left the place in perfect condition."

"That's because she was never here," he said. "She worked so many hours but couldn't make things work."

"Do you know where she moved?" I asked.

He shook his head. "Somewhere cheaper, I'm sure. Without a job, Chicago can be very expensive. This is one of the least expensive places that's still got all the security and stuff."

Yoli glanced down at her shoes as if embarrassed about living in the least expensive place.

"I'm sure I couldn't afford to live here," I said. "It's a nice place."

"Thanks. I work hard to keep it nice." His smile widened.

"And it shows," I said. "Are you sure she didn't leave any forwarding addresses or anything?"

He shook his head, but Yoli's head snapped up. "Actually, she did. I forgot until you mentioned it, but she left a note on the kitchen counter explaining where I could send anything that mistakenly came for her. I hadn't actually looked at it that hard. It's in the junk drawer. I can run upstairs and get it quick."

"That would be wonderful," I said, hope rising in my

chest. I turned to the maintenance guy and said, "Thank you for your help. Keep up the good work."

He beamed as Yoli, and I walked out of his office.

Yoli took the stairs two at a time, yelling back that she'd meet me in the lobby.

She must have been an expert stair runner because, by the time I was in the lobby, I only had to wait a minute or two before she returned holding a torn piece of paper with a forwarding address.

"Do you mind if I snap a picture of it?" I asked, pulling out my phone.

"Not at all," she said.

I took the photo and pulled it up to make sure it wasn't blurry. As I read the address, I almost gasped. The forwarding address was her father's house.

I tried my best not to give away my emotions and keep my hair from changing. The last thing I needed was to freak Yoli out.

"Thanks again," I said.

"Is something the matter?" Yoli asked, glancing at the paper. "Oh, Cliff Haven. Isn't that the small town your mom's from? Is that where you live now?"

"It is," I said.

"And you haven't seen Jasmine around?"

I shook my head, avoiding eye contact.

"Maybe she went on a vacation or something," Yoli offered. "Though if she didn't have the money to stay here, she probably couldn't afford a vacation. Ooh, or maybe she's crashing with friends. She needed a place to forward mail and stuff, but she didn't plan on going back to stay."

That made sense, though it didn't get me any closer to finding her.

"Thanks again for all your help," I said. "It was nice meeting you."

"You too," Yoli said. "I hope you find her."

"I do, too."

I walked across the road to Mona and asked her to take us to the law firm where Jasmine had worked.

Mona happily zoomed along the Chicago streets as I wondered what was next.

Jasmine had been fired from Gorvich's firm. According to the maintenance guy from her building, she hadn't been a very good attorney, but she got her dad out of jail on bail after he was arrested for murder the first time. That didn't suggest she was bad at it. Or maybe the judge was okay with it because Gus had an ankle tracker.

The law firm had a small empty parking lot off the side. The signs in front of the spots all said the same thing: Law Firm Parking Only, All Others Will Be Towed.

Mona parked in the spot closest to the door.

A sign I couldn't quite make out was taped to the inside of the door.

I hopped out and walked to the door.

Closed Indefinitely

I tried the door, but it was locked.

"Gahhhh!"

"Are you okay?" A man asked from the sidewalk that passed in front of the building.

"I'm fine," I said.

"Do you need a lawyer?"

"No. I'm looking for someone who worked here."

"I walk by here every morning. Maybe I've seen them."

This guy was probably a waste of time, but he was more of an option than I had otherwise.

I described Jasmine and her fancy car as he listened intently.

"I think I've seen the woman, but she never drove a car like that. Her car was a total beater." He shrugged. "But maybe she got a promotion or something, and I just didn't see her before they closed down indefinitely."

"How long ago did they close?" I asked. I'd assumed they'd closed because Gorvich had died.

"At least a week ago, if not longer." He glanced at the parking lot. "Your van is the first vehicle I've seen parked here in at least that long."

"Thanks," I said. "That's very helpful."

"No problem," he said. "I know this is pretty blunt, but can I get your number?"

I was so caught off guard I didn't think about controlling my hair.

My scalp tingled, and the man's eyes flickered to my head before he laughed nervously. "Uh, sorry, that was weird. I—uh—gotta go."

"Thank you," I yelled after him as he ran away down the sidewalk.

I slipped back into Mona and laid my forehead on the steering wheel.

"What am I missing?"

I wanted to call Jake and tell him what I found, but

he'd already made up his mind. Then a thought clicked into place.

I sat up and called Neve.

She answered on the first ring. "Ellie? What's up? Where are you?"

"I'm in Chicago," I said.

"Jake thought that might be the case," she replied. "He asked me if I knew where you were. I think he went by your house and got breakfast this morning. Katie, obviously, wasn't going to tell him."

"I know Jasmine had something to do with these murders," I said. "Has Jake watched the drone footage yet?"

"I don't know," Neve said. "If he has, he hasn't said anything."

"What about the evidence?" I asked. "Have you found anything that suggests Jasmine could be in on it?"

"I'm looking, but so far, nothing," she said. "Why are you so set on her having something to do with it?"

"The drone video shows a woman in the field with her chest exposed, and the breasts are fake."

"Okay, I know Jasmine has a large chest, but couldn't that be anyone?"

"There's also a video of the car she'd been driving parked near the trees," I said. "The trees where we found the kitty litter and wheelbarrow."

Neve cussed. "I'll talk to Jake, but is there anything else I can do?"

I thought about it for a minute. "Do you think you could run a plate for me?"

"Not directly," Neve said. "That's not exactly in my job description. But I do know someone who can."

"Perfect," I said. "Can you run the plate from Jasmine's car?"

"Do you have the plate number?"

Shoot. "I don't. Do you think there's any way you could get it from the evidence? I would bet the car is in one of the photos."

Neve sighed. "I'll see what I can do. But in the meantime, will you please be careful? Andrea's not there to protect you, and we need you to be the next Grand Witch. The alternative is way too grim to even consider."

"I'll be careful," I said. "But how did you know—"

"I'll let you know what I find."

Neve disconnected the call before I could ask how she knew Andrea wasn't with me.

21

Not sure what else to do, I headed back to Cliff Haven. I needed to think, so I drove myself. From what I could tell, Mona seemed relieved not to have to use her magic to get us home quickly.

"Thanks for all your help today," I said to Mona. "I couldn't do what I do without you."

Her RPMs increased a bit in reply.

"Now, I have to find Jasmine or get Jake to find her." I thought for a minute. "You would think Gus—in all his Gus-ness—would be eager to throw his daughter under the bus. But maybe he doesn't know she had anything to do with it. And if that's the case, it would mean Jasmine worked alone, and Gus—as horrible as he is—is innocent."

I watched as the city turned to fields. I was about to ask Mona to speed it up when my phone rang.

"Hello?" I said, putting the phone on speaker.

"Wow, it's loud there. Where are you?" Neve asked.

"Just driving back," I said. I drove Mona so often I

didn't think about how noisy she probably was. Especially on the interstate going her top non-magical driving speed of sixty-five miles per hour. "What did you find?"

"Jake watched the video. He'll probably be calling you soon."

As if on cue, Jake's face popped up on the screen. I'd call him back.

"I think he realized Jasmine has something to do with it," Neve continued. "Not that he'd give me the satisfaction of coming out and saying it."

"What about the car?" I asked. "Did you run the plate?"

"It was a rental," Neve said. "Jasmine rented it from a place in Iowa City."

"Has she returned it?"

"It was towed last night and is impounded. I tried to call the impound lot, but it was closed."

"Can you send me the address?" I asked. "Maybe I can find someone who will talk to me. Or at least get a peek at the car."

"That car could be a crime scene. Don't go touching it," Neve warned.

"I won't," I said.

"All right," she said. "I'll send you the address. And call Jake back. He's in my office staring me down."

I could hear Jake in the background mumble something.

"I'll call him right now. Thanks, Neve."

I disconnected, and the phone rang before I could even get to Jake's contact.

"I figured I'd save you the danger of calling while you're driving," Jake said.

"Well, hello to you, too."

"Are you going to the impound lot?"

"Yep," I said without giving him the opportunity to tell me not to.

"I'll meet you there," he said.

"I don't think Jasmine will be at the impound lot," I said. "You should try to find her and arrest her."

"Look at you calling the shots," Jake said with a touch of pride in his voice.

"I don't think Gus did it," I said. "I think she framed him because she was mad. She hasn't been employed for a while and didn't win cases when she was. She hasn't lived in her Chicago apartment for at least two months. Her forwarding address was Gus's house."

"Do you think she was staying with him?"

"No," I said. "But I think she's staying somewhere close. Do you know where they towed the car from?"

"I haven't been able to get in touch with anyone from the lot, but the lot is in Poppy Hills. My guess is she's somewhere close."

"She's somewhere close without a car or money," I said. "She can't hide out for long. My guess is she'll try to break into Gus's house eventually. Do you still have officers there?"

"Yes," Jake said. "But I'll make sure they're on the lookout."

"Have them do a thorough check of the place one more time. Just in case she has a good hiding spot, you know?"

"Anything else?" He was only half-joking.

I thought for a second. "Gus might be a good source of information. Even if it is just with the house. He probably knows all the good hiding spots." I paused. "Otherwise, I'll let you know if I find anything from the impound lot."

"Sounds good," Jake said. "Oh, and one more thing."

"Yeah?"

"I'm sorry for being harsh before."

"It's okay," I said. "I know the wedding has you all stressed. But it'll be over soon, and everything will finally calm down."

"Uh—yeah—the wedding." He sounded like he didn't realize that was the source of his stress until I pointed it out. "Either way, I shouldn't have taken my stress out on you."

"All is forgiven," I said. "Let's find Jasmine and get her behind bars before she hurts anyone else."

***

Mona got me to the impound lot in record time. "Sorry we had to use your magic so much," I said. "I appreciate it, though."

Her engine revved, letting me know she was perfectly okay.

The impound lot was a big parking lot surrounded by a tall chain-link fence with barbed wire on the top. It was also magical.

I'd become much more aware of magical places since I found out they existed. This one differed from most, though. Most magical places were invisible to the non-magical eye. But this one was visibly an impound lot and magically a dealership, too. Very similar to the dealership where I'd received Mona. That was the first time I'd met Gerald.

My heart constricted in my chest.

I checked my phone. I hadn't heard from Xander, so I sent him a quick message.

How is everything?

His response came almost instantly.

XANDER

He's still holding on. How's the case?

I think we figured out who did it. We just need to find her.

Be careful. Andrea should be back soon.

I'll be careful. Let me know if anything changes.

I will.

I put the phone in the designer purse and walked to the dealership door, which was unlocked and open for business.

"Hello, how can we help you?" A receptionist witch asked when I walked through the door.

"I would like to talk to someone regarding the impound lot," I said.

"Yeah, no one's around for the lot," she said. "We're a dealership."

"Right," I said. "Is there someone I could call?"

"The impound staff is off today, and they don't much like being bothered on their days off."

"What about the boss? Is the boss available?"

"She's off too."

I glanced around. The salespeople stared at me.

"I can take a message if you'd like. She can call you when she gets in tomorrow."

An idea popped into my head. I raised my voice slightly for the rest of the people in the room to hear. "I'm Ellie Vanderwick." I rattled off my number, but she stopped me.

"As in those Vanderwicks?" she interrupted as the others murmured to themselves.

"The Grand Witch ones?"

She nodded.

"Yep," I said. "I'm next in line."

She looked like she was going to pass out.

"But it's okay. I can wait until tomorrow. I don't want to put anyone out on their day off."

"No, no," she said. "I'm sure the boss would be only too happy to talk to you. Let me call her."

She only said about five words, two of them being Ellie and Vanderwick, before she hung up and said, "The boss will be here in two minutes."

A minute and a half later, a witch, probably in her mid-forties, wearing a pencil skirt and tight blouse, walked in and introduced herself as the property owner. "What can I help you with?"

"I'm helping the non-magical police on a case in Cliff

Haven, and I think a car you recently towed has a connection."

"Oh, sure," she said, leading me out of the dealership office and over to the impound office. "What car are you interested in?"

I told her the make, model, and color. "I believe it was towed last night at the request of a rental car company."

"Yes, I know exactly which one you're talking about," she said.

"Can you tell me where your driver picked it up?"

She turned on a computer and started clicking through a program that seemed to keep all their records. "Here it is." She grabbed a piece of paper and wrote the address.

I didn't need her to hand it to me before I realized where it was.

"Are you sure that's correct?" I asked when she handed me the slip of paper.

"Unless the driver wrote something down wrong, yes." She glanced at the computer, then back at me. "Is everything okay?"

I sucked in a breath. "Everything's fine."

"Can I do anything else for you?" she asked. "I feel terrible we gave you such a hard time at the dealership. If we had known who you were—"

"It's okay," I said, not loving how it felt to be treated kindly only because of my name. "Can I go out and look at the car?"

"Sure," she said. "I think the dealership is coming to pick it up tomorrow."

"I would venture to guess they won't have the opportunity," I said. "The police will want to examine it as a crime scene."

"Oh." Her eyes widened. "Okay."

We walked out to the middle of the lot, where the car sat between two trucks. I leaned over and peeked inside the back window without touching the glass. It didn't look like anything had happened.

I walked to the other side, did the same thing, and then repeated the action in the front two windows.

It wasn't until I reached the driver's side that I noticed something shiny poking out from between the center console and the seat. It looked like the tip of a knife.

"Looks like my suspicions were right," I said.

I texted Jake with the best possible picture of the knife tip.

"Is there anything I can do to assist in the process?" the boss witch asked.

"Just make sure no one comes in and messes with the car before the police arrive." I started toward the gate. "I need to get home. This car was towed from my driveway."

22

Mona drove home as quickly as I would have expected. My mind raced through the possibilities. She couldn't hide in the house—there was no way the house would have let a murderer inside. Unless the murderer didn't want to kill me but rather stay hidden.

She could also be in the barn. There wasn't protection magic in the barn that I knew of.

The number of tents had diminished from my field, leaving only a few here and there. She could easily hide in a tent.

Katie and the gang had already cleaned up and cleared out. A note on the counter said Katie took Penelope home so she wouldn't be alone.

Jasmine might have come in during breakfast and hidden somewhere. And without Penelope there, she could still be inside undetected.

"Esme?" I whispered when I opened the back door. If

Esme was around, she might know if I had a squatter. But she was nowhere to be found.

I took a deep breath. The only way to find out was to look.

I pulled out my phone to send Jake a message, but it was dead.

I plugged it into the charging cord on the counter and waited. It made no sense to search for a murderer without backup on the way.

But before the phone charged enough to power on, Jasmine walked into the kitchen wearing my robe and slippers, whistling a familiar tune. Her hair was wet as if she'd just gotten out of the shower.

"Hi," I said when she caught sight of me.

"What are you doing here?" she asked as if I was the one out of place in this situation.

"This is my house," I said.

"This is the others's house."

I wanted to yell at her, but Deb's warning about Jasmine and Esme's words about killing people with kindness both came back to me. With Jasmine not in her right mind, this was likely the perfect situation to use the tactic.

"Did you enjoy breakfast?" I asked as she opened the fridge and started digging through the leftovers.

"It was delicious," she said. "Did they have any pancakes left over?"

"I'm not sure," I said. "I could make you some."

I glanced at my phone. It still hadn't turned on.

If everything else failed, I could teleport, but that might also allow Jasmine to get away.

"I'm okay," she said, emerging from the refrigerator holding a gun. "But some coffee would be great."

She didn't point the gun at me, but she was holding it with her finger on the trigger.

"Where did you get a gun?" I made the coffee very slowly while keeping her in my peripheral vision.

"Does it matter where I got it?" Jasmine asked, glancing down at the shiny piece of metal in her hand.

"No, I suppose it doesn't," I said. "Are you enjoying the house?"

"Oh yes," she said, pacing by the back door. "This home is lovely."

I had no idea why the house wasn't doing anything to get her out of there. Though, it wasn't the first time I'd had my life threatened in this very kitchen. Maybe I needed to rethink how much my house actually protected me.

"When did you get here?" I turned on the coffee maker and stepped toward my phone.

"Last night," she said, also stepping toward my phone. "My father's house is under construction. I slept in a tent with a very nice woman. When I woke up, my car and all my money had been stolen. Thankfully, your friends were making breakfast, and the woman I spent the night with in the tent bought me a plate."

"That sounds great," I said. "When did they say your father's house will be ready for you to return?"

"Are you trying to get rid of me?" Her voice went from chill to angry and she lifted the gun slightly so the barrel was aimed at my torso.

"No," I said. "Just trying to make conversation."

"My father murdered people," she said, her voice back to chill. "Now he's in jail."

"That's horrible. You must be devastated."

"They deserved to die," she said, pointing the gun away from me again. "One threatened to burn down my father's house, and the other fired me for no reason. Both of them wanted their shot with the others, but my father couldn't let that happen."

"Did your dad take matters into his own hands so he could meet the others?" I asked, going along with her story.

"My father hates the others," she said. "I've tried to tell him how kind they are, but he never listens to me."

The coffee maker went off with three beeps. "I'm going to get you coffee, okay?"

She didn't respond, but also didn't aim the gun at me again.

"It was pretty gruesome," she said. "Stabbing people produces a lot of blood. But it's easy to get off when you're not wearing clothes."

"Do you want cream or sugar?" I asked.

"Black," she said. "The kitty litter came in handy. I knew dad kept it in the garage for spills."

"Where did he put all the dirty kitty litter after it soaked up the blood?" I asked, handing her the cup of coffee.

I would have tried to scald her with it, but as she took it, the gun barrel was pointed at me again. With her finger on the trigger, it was too risky.

"Scooped it right into the trunk of the car," Jasmine said.

I waited for her to take a sip. Maybe that would give me an opening. An opening for what? I wasn't certain.

"Why would your dad have been naked in the first place?"

"To accept the aliens," she said. "You have to be completely free of anything from this world for them to take you."

"And he wanted them to take him?"

"No," she said, turning to look out the window.

This was my chance. I needed something to neutralize her.

The junk basket was right next to my phone. Inside was a flashlight that needed new batteries. An idea popped into my mind.

"Men are ridiculously enamored with the female body. They practically didn't even notice the knife. If they'd have just let me have the aliens, they might have lived."

"Men can be very single-minded regarding that, can't they?" I reached my hand slowly toward the junk basket, wrapping my fingers around the flashlight and pulling it back toward me.

"It makes things much easier for women like us." She turned quickly and I thought I was caught. But then she began to examine me starting with my face, then my chest, then looked down at her cleavage. "Well, maybe more for women like me." She laughed. "You know, you can have procedures to make those bigger, right?"

"Really? Is that how yours turned out so nice?" I hated myself for continuing down this path with her, but I needed to wait for the perfect opening to enact my plan.

"You just have to find a man to pay for them."

"Why not pay for them yourself?" I asked. "You have such a nice car, a good job, and a bunch of money."

She laughed. "It's convincing, isn't it? I mean, look at you. You're all dressed up. In that outfit, you look like a millionaire. Unlike when you wear your athleisure clothes."

Funnily enough, I was a millionaire, regardless of what I wore. But I wouldn't tell her that. "You don't have a bunch of money?"

"I didn't but my father did," she said. "Too bad he didn't want to share. Soon, he'll go to prison, die, and I'll inherit everything. He was too stupid to draw up a will. Which means I'll get it all, no matter what."

"Is he sick? Is that why you think he'll die?" I asked, my voice as caring as I could make it. I held the flashlight below the counter, out of Jasmine's view. My objective was to take it completely apart.

"Not yet, he's not," she said. "But I bet I can get someone to help me out. Maybe a prison guard."

Her laughter echoed through the room, sending chills down my spine.

"Did you see your father kill those men?" I asked. "That must have been scary for you."

"He could never. He didn't have the nerve to do something like that," Jasmine said. "And why send a man to do a woman's job?"

"I don't understand," I said.

"It's a secret," she whispered.

This was my opening. I sucked in a breath. "If you tell me your secret, I'll give you my alien attracter."

Her eyes widened. "Your what?"

"Isn't that why you were in the trees that night naked? You wanted to meet the aliens?"

"They were supposed to take me with them, but stupid Marty scared them away."

"I can help," I said, holding my hand out with all the pieces of the palm-sized silver flashlight. "I have all the parts. That's where I was. I just got back from finding the last piece."

"You can't be serious," she said. "I've been looking for this. We all have."

"I think the others led me to the last piece because I gave them my property," I said.

"And you'll give it to me?"

"I think you deserve it after all you've been through."

She nodded. "It was so hard. Marty was so heavy and the wheelbarrow kept tipping over. And that stupid Gorvich actually thought he had a chance with me."

"Just give me the gun and you can have all the pieces," I said.

She glanced at the gun in her hand as if she had forgotten it was there.

"I'm sure you know how to put it back together much better than me."

Her gaze went from the gun to the pieces in my hand. She put the gun on the counter and slid it to me.

I snatched it up and handed her the pieces of the flashlight.

She instantly went to work trying to put it back together. With her distracted, I picked up my phone and called Jake. When I heard him say hello, I said, "Do you need any help with that, Jasmine?"

"Why are you shouting?" she said. "I'm right here. And no. I have to do it myself if I want them to come for me."

Now all I needed to do was stall. And if all else failed, I was the one with the gun.

Thankfully, Jasmine wasn't very good at assembling things and before I knew it, Jake burst in with his gun drawn as if we were in a movie. "Jasmine, don't move. You're under arrest."

Jasmine looked up at him from her position on the floor. "What are you talking about? I can't be under arrest. I'm not even a citizen of this planet."

"Stand up and put your hands on your head," Jake said.

She stood slowly, clutching the pieces of the flashlight to her chest. "What are you arresting me for?"

"Murder among other things," Jake said. "Turn around."

She did so, and another officer hurried up to her. As he handcuffed her, all the piece of the flashlight fell on the ground.

"No!" Jasmine yelled. "That was mine!"

"It's okay," I said. "The others know about you. If they come back, they'll find you."

Jasmine turned to look at me with tears in her eyes, but said nothing else.

As they led her out the door, the officer reader her rights.

"Here," I said, handing Jake the gun. "I don't know where it came from, but she had this."

"And you got it away from her?" Jake asked.

"I tricked her," I said. "But she practically confessed to the murders. Oh, and the missing kitty litter will probably still be in the trunk of her rental car."

"I have a feeling she'll try for the insanity plea," Jake said. "That might have been her plan all along. Who knows? You did a good job. Looks like I need to do a better job listening to you, huh?"

I shrugged. "I guess when I get a feeling about something, yeah."

"Do you think Gus was in on it?"

I shook my head. "No. I think she set it up to look like he was."

"You might have to testify to what happened today," Jake said.

"Happily."

"I'll leave you to it." Jake left, and I took a deep breath. "Let me know if you need anything."

I locked the door after he left.

Another case solved.

I needed a nap before I went to pick up Penelope.

Too bad, as I was headed up the stairs to my room, the doorbell rang.

23

Part of me didn't want to answer, but maybe someone needed help.

When I opened the door, I gasped.

Almost every witch and warlock I knew stood on my deck, down the steps, and in my yard.

I say almost because Xander was noticeably missing.

"Can we come in?" Renée asked.

Lucy smiled at me.

"Sure," I said.

They filed in and went to the dining room, each saying hello as they passed.

Bernardo, Andrea, the entire magical council, Harriet and her foster dog, Wix, Lucy, Renée, and many others packed in so tightly I almost couldn't make it through.

Once I was in the dining room, at the head of the table where a seat had been left open for me, I sat.

"Thank you for inviting us in," Renée said. "We have a crucial matter to discuss today."

Would they tell me they didn't want me as Grand

Witch anymore? The thought of not being the Grand Witch now seemed worse than the thought of being the Grand Witch. I didn't want them to take it away from me.

"We need to talk about your mother," Renée said.

This snapped me out of my thoughts. "My mother?"

"Yes," Renée said. "We understand Gerald is in his last moments of life and that his spell—illegally cast—to remove your mother's memories will not be restored before he dies."

How they knew all this was beyond me, but I nodded. "He didn't want healing either."

"We suspect that is because if he were healed, he'd spend the rest of his life in a magical prison for all the illegal spells he's cast over the years," Lars Templeton—the President of the Magical Governing Council—said.

That made sense.

"We've come to discuss whether she will get her memories back at all," Renée continued. "We've been meeting about this for the past week, trying to come up with ways to return her memories while doing no damage to her brain."

My heartbeat quickened. Had they come up with a solution?

"We believe we can make it happen," Lucy said excitedly.

"You do?" I asked. "How?"

"It'll be a meticulous process that will probably take multiple witches and warlocks and a few weeks to perform," Renée said.

"Let me stop you right there," I said. "Why are you

doing this? Is it so she can become the Grand Witch instead of me?"

No one spoke. Several people shot glances at others.

"You can tell me," I said. "Please, just tell me."

Renée took a breath. "We have a stipulation to agreeing to fix her memory."

"And?" I asked. I wanted to yell—spit it out already!

"We will only do this if you agree to become the Grand Witch," Renée finished. "We, under no circumstances, want Emily to become the Grand Witch of the States."

Part of me was offended on behalf of Emily, but the other part of me understood. They only knew the Emily she was—the person who gave up her magic and memories at the drop of a hat. It didn't matter to them that she'd done it to protect someone she loved. Giving up our magic was apparently the worst thing we could ever do.

"Ellie, we know this is hard for you," Lucy said. "You might not feel ready, but we need you."

"And we think you're more than ready," Lars said.

"You do?" This surprised me.

"We do." Renée smiled.

"Then we have a deal," I said.

A chorus of gasps sounded.

"Actually, no, hold on," I said.

Everyone seemed to hold their breath.

"I don't want you to restore Emily's memory," I said. "But I will become Grand Witch of the States."

A joint exhale of relief filled the air. They thought I would fight with them over this. And maybe I would have a few weeks before. But now, I was ready.

"Are you sure you don't want us to return her memories?" Renée asked.

I nodded. "I'm one hundred percent certain. Emily wouldn't want that, either."

"Great." Lars stood. "Then we'll be on our way. Your ceremony will take place in three weeks. Until then, stay safe and out of trouble."

"I can't promise anything." I laughed.

He didn't seem to think it was very funny.

Several people left right away, while others stayed to chat. Bernardo didn't stay back. He probably knew Xander, and I were dating. And now that I would be the Grand Witch, I couldn't date either of them since they were both on the magical board.

I sighed. It was a sacrifice I had to make.

I yawned, and Lucy said, "Okay, everyone, let's get out of Ellie's hair. She's had a big day and probably wants to get some rest."

I said goodbye to everyone individually, giving lots of hugs and promising to see them later.

"Wow, that was intense," Esme said after I closed the door and returned to the living room. "Are you doing okay?"

"Yeah," I said. "I'm all right. Sad that Xander and I can't be together, but otherwise, I'm okay."

"You're the true embodiment of a Vanderwick witch. You know that?" Esme said.

Pride filled my chest. "I should probably go to bed."

"Hold on," Esme said, glancing behind her at the wall. "I think someone needs to speak to you."

"What do you mean?" I stood. "Is someone still outside?"

"No, no. Sit down. Here he comes." Esme moved a couple of inches to the side, and another ghost appeared beside her.

In all his previously handsome glory, Gerald floated around next to Esme.

"Does that mean you've passed?" I asked.

My phone chirped from the kitchen. That was probably Xander telling me as much.

"I can't stay long," Gerald said. "They made special accommodations so I could see you."

"Then hurry and say what you need to," Esme said.

"Always the pushy one, even in death," Gerald teased.

Esme rolled her eyes.

"First, I'd like to thank you for heeding my wishes. You could have healed me without my consent. I would have been furious, but I would have been alive."

I didn't interrupt. There was no use fighting about whether being alive or dead was preferable in his situation.

"Second, promise me you'll take care of Xander. That boy loves you, and I know you love him. He deserves all the happiness in the world."

Gerald's form flickered a bit. "I'm running out of time. There's one more thing."

I was on the edge of my seat. "What? What is it?"

As if he was on a cell phone and going through a tunnel, I only caught a handful of his words. "Sorry—be—no—what —careful—help—Emily." Then he flickered out of sight.

"What did he say?" I asked Esme standing from the sofa.

"I don't know," Esme said. "Something about Emily and help and careful and he's sorry?"

"Do you think he was apologizing for not bringing Emily's memories back?" I asked.

Esme shrugged. "I don't know. Maybe."

I slumped on the couch. I should have gotten my phone to check Xander's text message, but how could I comfort him when I was a mess myself?

"You did everything you could," Esme said. "Don't cry."

For the second time that night, the doorbell rang.

My jaw dropped when I opened the door.

Before I could make sense of anything, Emily wrapped me in the biggest hug ever.

"What? How?"

"Oh, Ellie," Emily said. "I'm so sorry. I didn't know what you were talking about at the hospital. Of course, I would have wanted to know you. I do want to know you." She pulled back and looked me up and down, tears streaking down her face. "You're even more beautiful than I thought was possible."

"Wait, where's Eloise? How did you get here?" I asked. "And what are you talking about?"

"She's at the hospital with Xander," Emily said. "They're mourning their father's death, and I couldn't wait to see you."

"Esme?" I asked. "Grandma?"

"I thought—didn't she—"

Esme floated to the entryway, ghostly tears running down her translucent cheeks. "You're back."

"I'm sorry I left," Emily said. "I wish I could have stayed with you."

"You could have," Esme said. "We could have fought Monroe together."

"I know that now," Emily said. "But I was scared and young. I didn't want anything to happen to you or Ellie."

"I understand why you did it," Esme said. "And I don't hold any blame."

"Whoa, whoa, whoa," I said. "What is going on right now? How did you know where I live? How are you even here?"

Emily turned her attention back to me. "I have my memory back."

"You what? Did the spell die because Gerald died? Do all spells die—or revert—when a person dies?" I asked, a mixture of confusion and joy spreading through me. "I need a bit more information here."

"Gerald must have known he was about to die," Emily said. "He did it just before. I heard his heartbeat monitor beeping. Then the sound turned to a solid tone."

Gratefulness spread through me. I only wish I had known, so I could have expressed my thanks when I saw Gerald.

I let my emotions change my hair.

Emily smiled. "I wondered if you'd have the family hair. And it seems you've learned to control it."

"Faster than you did," Esme joked.

Emily beamed at me. She was radiant. Her hair was a shimmery white, and her skin glowed.

"After everything gets sorted, can Eloise and I come to live here with you?" Emily asked, her voice nervous.

"Everything like Gerald's funeral and stuff?" I asked. "And this house belongs to you more than me."

"No," Esme and Emily said in unison, then laughed together.

"This is your home," Emily said. "I gave up my claim to anything regarding the Vanderwick name when I decided to alter memories. I may be in trouble magically and non-magically for my decisions. But once everything is sorted, I'd love to come back and at least visit."

"There will be no visiting," I said. "You can absolutely come live here. As long as Eloise is okay with it."

"She's a pre-teen," Emily said. "She'll get used to it, eventually."

"I assume you have your magic back," Esme asked.

"Just as strong as the day I gave it away," Emily said.

Esme shook her head but smiled nonetheless.

In the distance, the lights of a police car came into view.

Emily's eyes widened. "I didn't think he'd come so quickly."

"You think Jake knows you're here?" I asked. "Maybe he's coming to win your heart back."

Emily faltered at Jake's name, then seemed to regain her composure. "I'm going to hide. Don't tell him I'm here. Not yet, okay?"

She ran past me into the house and up the stairs. I could imagine her as a girl doing the same thing, running up to her bedroom.

Esme didn't budge. "I'll stay with you. I want to know what Jake has to say."

"Why would he care if she erased her memory?" I asked. "Do you really think she'll be in trouble?"

"I think we're about to find out," Esme said as Jake pulled into the driveway and practically flew out of his car before it stopped.

"Are you okay?" Jake asked. "Is she here?"

"I'm fine," I said. "Is who here?"

Jake gathered me in a massive hug. "I was so worried. When I realized—I don't even know what happened—but when the cloud in my mind cleared, I knew I had to get here before she did."

"Who?" I asked again. I assumed he was talking about Emily but didn't want to give her away if he wasn't.

"Emily," he said, pulling away from me. "I believe Emily is alive, and if she is, I think she'll try to contact you soon."

I wanted to see the expression on Esme's face, but Jake couldn't see her. It would look strange if I glanced over. "Why is that a problem? Isn't that good news?"

"Ellie, I don't know how to explain this other than to tell you I think Emily messed with my head or my memory or something."

"She messed with your memory?"

"Mine and the entire town's," Jake said. "But then it was like a switch flipped. I was in the police station, and a fog lifted. I felt it. Everyone around me felt it. And pieces started clicking into place."

My mind spun, trying to figure out what he was talking about. "I don't understand."

"Emily must have cast a spell to make us forget, but now we remember. We remember everything."

He gathered me back into his arms.

"Jake, what is going on?" I asked, pushing him away gently. "Why are you hugging me so much?"

"I was wrong, Ellie," he said, his blue eyes focused on mine. "The reason you have blue eyes and love crispy-edged pancakes, it's because you're my daughter. Emily took away my memories of us—uh—you know. But we did. And she told me about you. I was ecstatic. But she said she couldn't stay. I tried to get her to stay, but she wouldn't. Then I forgot. Magically."

My breath was stuck in my chest. I couldn't inhale or exhale. Jake just told me he was my dad. "Say something," Jake said. "I know this is a lot. I'm sorry you grew up in foster homes. I would have been there, I swear."

Esme whispered in my ear, "Ellie, it's okay. Find your center. Find your breath."

I finally sucked in some air. "I—I can't believe it."

"Me neither," Jake said.

I took a step toward him and let him hug me again. I had a dad. And a mom. And a sister. And a future step-mom.

"I love you," Jake said. "And I am so proud of you."

"I love you too," I said. "I'm sorry Emily did this. I'm sure she had a reason."

"She had a reason, all right," Jake said, pulling away from me. "She erased our memories because she was about to go to jail for murder."

Esme and I both gasped. Apparently, Esme hadn't regained her memories like Jake had. Maybe she only had the information she had when she died.

"She didn't murder anyone," I said. "How could you say that?"

"Because I found her best friend dead," Jake said. "And all the evidence pointed to Emily."

"No." I took a step back. "That's not true."

"It's an open case. A case I need to solve. That's the other reason I hurried over. She could be dangerous. If she killed her best friend, she could easily kill someone else she loves. Like you."

A gurgled laugh came from my throat. "She wouldn't kill me. She's not a killer. She's my mom."

"I know that's what every orphan wants to think—that their parents are perfect—but that's not always the case."

I wanted to slam the door in his face. I loved him and was ecstatic that he was my father, but I couldn't let him stand here and tell me Emily was a murderer. She didn't even remember anything. If she was trying to hide from something, wouldn't she have kept her memories and erased everyone else's?

"I'll stay in case she comes here," Jake said.

"How will Georgia feel about that?" I asked.

"Georgia and I broke up," Jake said. "I realized when you told me that I was stressed because of the wedding, it wasn't because I was stressed because of the wedding. It was because I was stressed about marrying the wrong person."

My feelings were a jumbled mess inside my chest. Like a beehive where all the exits had been blocked, and the bees frantically bumped around, trying to escape.

"You don't need to stay," I said. "Andrea is coming back tonight and will be here to protect me from here on out. I accepted the position as Grand Witch of the States."

Jake stood staring at me for a bit longer, then nodded. "Okay, but you keep your phone charged and on you at all times. If Emily shows up, call me right away."

"Okay," I lied. "I will."

"Maybe we can go to Katie's and get some of our favorite pancakes tomorrow." Jake started toward his car.

"I'd love to," I said, waving goodbye.

Once he was out of sight, I closed the door and bolted up the stairs.

"Which room was hers?" I asked Esme. How had I never asked that before? How had I never been curious about which room my mom had grown up in?

"None of these," Esme said. "Follow me."

We took a severe right turn when we hit the top of the stairs, and Esme pointed up.

A small square I'd never noticed before was in the ceiling with a pull cord coming down. "Was this always here?"

Esme shrugged. "My memories are still really fuzzy. I think ghosts might be affected by this kind of magic differently than the living."

I pulled the cord, and the hatch opened easily, a ladder slowly emerging and unfolding until it hit the floor to the right of the top of the staircase.

"Emily? Are you up there?" I asked, climbing the ladder carefully. "Jake's gone. I didn't tell him anything."

The room was perfectly preserved. Pictures of Emily and Jake and friends I didn't recognize covered the wallpapered walls. Her bed—a four-poster with gorgeous white silk draping that contrasted against the dark wood—still had pillows that looked like they'd just been fluffed.

A bookcase covered an entire wall with a fair mix of magazines, classics, and books I assumed were from magical authors. I could have looked around the room for days, examining every feature. It was almost like I could feel my mother's teenage presence here. But, unfortunately, her actual presence wasn't here.

"She's gone," I said.

"Again," Esme said.

I walked to the desk and found a note hastily written.

Ellie,
It's not goodbye. It's only until next time. I can't wait to get to know you.
I love you,
Mom

All your questions will be answered in the final book of the Magical Mane Mystery Series, coming soon! Make sure to preorder it now!

ACKNOWLEDGMENTS

As always, thanks goes to my family, friends, and God.

My writing friends are the best. They build me up every single day and I am so thankful for them.

Without my readers, I'd be out of a job. Thank YOU so much for reading my books—I hope they have given you a bit of escape and joy.

A huge thanks to my beta readers, ARC readers, social media sharers, and fellow authors. You are all integral to my success.

ABOUT THE AUTHOR

Stella Bixby is a native Coloradan who loves to snowboard, pluck at the guitar, and play board games with her family. She was once a volunteer firefighter and a park ranger, but now spends most of her time making up stories and trying to figure out what to cook for dinner.

Connect with Stella on Facebook, Twitter, and Instagram @StellaBixby.

Stella loves to hear from her readers!
www.stellabixby.com

Spelunking Speculations: Book 5

Festival Fiasco: Book 6

Jamboree Justice: Book 7

Cosmic Conspiracy: Book 8